T0114521

Memoirs of the Moon Dragon

The Maligrandé and the Source of Life

D. W. Middleton

Order this book online at www.trafford.com
or email orders@trafford.com

Most Trafford titles are also available at major online book retailers.

Printed in the United States of America.

ISBN: 978-1-4251-1091-8 (sc)
ISBN: 978-1-4669-4802-0 (e)

Library of Congress Control Number: 2012912620

Trafford rev. 09/27/2012

 www.trafford.com

North America & international
toll-free: 1 888 232 4444 (USA & Canada)
phone: 250 383 6864 ♦ fax: 812 355 4082

This book is dedicated to my two loving girls,
Swee-Gim and Elise.
Your faith and encouragement brings out the best
in me . . . God bless you both.

Contents

Birth of the Maligrandé

he dragon thought back and chuckled to himself. All those years behind him had left tales that would be told throughout eternity. It was all about instinct really. Everything—all of it. When it all boiled down, the centuries had taught him one thing—instinct. Every living thing has it, and you can get anything to do almost anything, if you know how its instincts work. Waldo's instinct as a country lad was to catch every rabbit he saw, and that's why the dragon sent the Black Rabbit to lure him, and lure him, it did!

The dragon chuckled to himself again . . . how something so simple could be the catalyst for so many things, but the fact was, Waldo was his whole reason for being. It was truly amazing that it had all started with something as simple as an unsuspecting lad deciding to follow his instinct, and chase a Black Rabbit that disappears into the ground. It was instinct that told Waldo there must be a rabbit hole around here somewhere. It was instinct that told him, wives' tales, when all he could find was a mysterious looking ring of red and white spotted toadstools. It was even instinct that told him that nothing will happen if I step into the toadstool ring, that toadstool ring stuff is all a bunch of gobbledygook. It was instinct that drove him to prove that point.

Instinct, that's what it all came down to. The dragon smiled to himself, lowered his head, and dozed off to sleep.

As soon as Waldo stepped into the toadstool ring the ground beneath his feet began to shimmer. He sank and fell straight through. It was as if he had just jumped out of an aeroplane. Truly, it had all happened so quickly. One second he was standing on firm ground, the next he was high in the sky, free falling through the air without a parachute. Looking down he could see the ground far beneath hurtling towards him. Waldo's heart raced as he realised the futility and inevitability of his situation. He was falling, faster and faster . . . he screamed, "Arrrrrrrgggghhhhhh!" It was to no avail. The ground thousands of meters below just kept rushing towards him as his body was buffeted in the wind. The wind was the only thing that was helping to break his fall. Waldo's whole body pounded as he was devoured with panic. He waved his outstretched arms and legs to try to slow himself down, but it was of no use. Waldo continued to fall—faster and faster!

As the ground got closer and closer, Waldo prepared to die. He was falling for what seemed like an eternity. As the objects on the ground grew larger and larger, his peripheral vision grew smaller and smaller, he braced himself. Waldo screamed out in a long blood-curdling howl, as he realised these would be the last few seconds before his very short life was over. His face was white with terminal thoughts, as the promise of an inevitable end engulfed him. Surely, the imminent and sudden impact with the ground, would bring his death. His life flashed before his eyes. The ground was just meters from his face now, and there was nothing to be done.

It would all be over soon . . . then it was! It was in mid scream that his body came to a sudden halt. It was surprisingly smooth, like the magnetic break on a free-falling ride in an amusement park. There was no jolt; he was simply pulled to a halt in an instant. Waldo found himself in disbelief. His body was now being suspended horizontally in mid air. He was stationary, just a few meters from the ground. Then, ever so slowly, his body was turned a full ninety degrees so that his feet pointed toward the ground, and ever so gently, he was lowered to the ground. He was back on solid ground again, and he was alive!

Waldo nearly fainted in his overwhelming relief! His body now drenched in sweat and his legs wobbly and weak. He could feel his heart racing as it pounded inside his chest. His face started to turn pink again, as finally, the blood rushed back to it. His body shook all over. Waldo steadied himself as he took a good look around. He could barely believe his eyes. Still in shock, his head started spinning . . . so many questions. How did he fall so far and with such speed and not die? How did he end up standing on the ground? What stopped his fall? What held him in the air? What rotated him so gently? Waldo looked up . . . there was nothing there, nothing but kilometres of clear sky above.

What was this place? Never anything more beautiful and serene had he seen. The trees were green. Flowers were blooming everywhere. The sun was warm. It shone from high in the sky above. He could hear the trickle of a stream. Butterflies and insects flew in the warm air. There was a path beneath his feet that led from the trees where he stood, into an open clearing. The clearing was drenched in bright sunlight. It drizzled in the haze, and he likened it to that of a warm day in late spring. It was quite clear to Waldo, that he had never been anywhere like this before. In fact, even though it had many similarities to Earth, he knew, that this was a completely different place.

In time Waldo would find out, that the myths about stepping into magic rings of toadstools and disappearing, whilst partly true, had nothing to do with magic. In fact, magic was a term created by humans, on Earth, to explain such mysteries. Surprisingly, never once did anyone suspect that whenever things happened, 'like magic' that they were merely being subject to the creative use of yet unknown to them, advanced technologies. Indeed, in this case, it was the use of an intergalactic transgression portal, that had brought Waldo here.

Needless to say, to Waldo, his situation was somewhat overwhelming. Waldo's first feelings were, to get back home now. He felt and clawed the air frantically where he stood, looking for a way back. It was of course no use. There was nothing to be felt or clawed but air. It was utterly hopeless! Whatever brought him here, there was now no means he could use to get himself back. Waldo's heart sank—he was trapped!

What should he do? He sank to the ground in complete and utter despair. It was then that he heard a scurrying sound, as you do when a small animal runs across dried leaves. Waldo instinctively looked up. He half expected a snake or a lizard, but it wasn't. Instead it was the Black Rabbit sitting just a few feet from his folded legs. The Black Rabbit's nose wiggled as he sniffed the air for danger. Waldo kept very still for there was something odd about this rabbit. For a start, it had what looked like a small round crystal ball hanging around its neck. Its movements weren't quite as smooth as they should have been either, but still remarkable for an android, which unknown to Waldo, is what the Black Rabbit actually was.

The Black Rabbit stood on its hind legs, folded its paws in front and said, "Are you the Maligrandé?"

Waldo exclaimed, "You can talk!"

"Are you the Maligrandé?" asked the Black Rabbit again impatiently.

"The Maligrandé?" asked Waldo.

"Yes the Maligrandé!" exclaimed the Black Rabbit. "Are you thick or something?"

"I don't think so," said Waldo still stunned.

"Mmm. No matter. We will find out soon enough," snorted the Black Rabbit.

"I just want to go back home!" exclaimed Waldo.

"Well you can't!" snapped the Black Rabbit.

"Then why am I here?" asked Waldo.

The Black Rabbit gave a heavy sigh. "To find out if you are the Maligrandé of course!"

"How do I do that?" asked Waldo.

The Black Rabbit retorted sarcastically, "You are stupid aren't you?"

"Look . . . Just follow this path and eventually it will lead you to The Great Book of Knowledge. If you haven't already found out by then, just ask it to tell you how to find out if you are the Maligrandé," replied the Black Rabbit dismissively.

With that, the Black Rabbit clasped the crystal transgression orb that was hanging around his neck in his paws, and in an instant became a shimmering wave, and disappeared completely. From this somewhat brash encounter with the Black Rabbit, Waldo gained at least a faint glimmer of hope that one day he might be able to return home. He mused to himself aloud, "If only I can find one of those crystals, maybe I can use it to shimmer back; hopefully, before anyone misses me." Waldo had no idea just how he might go about finding a crystal like that, but nevertheless, he was filled with optimism. Waldo was sure that sooner or later, he would indeed find one. He would then be able to return home. Just in time for afternoon tea he thought.

"Well, at least I have a plan now," Waldo thought to himself. So he set off following the worn dirt path that the rabbit pointed to. Waldo felt relieved. He was now becoming calm and relaxed. Waldo stopped. He took some time to take in this marvellous place. It was indeed a most beautiful land, that entrapped him. Never had he seen such an idyllic place. It was awash in a sea of colours and light. Birds were in abundance of many colourful varieties, most of which he had never seen before. There were many butterflies and flying insects, some strange to him. They fluttered and buzzed from flower to flower, all across the carpet of colour, that lay outstretched before him.

As he set off, Waldo pondered where the path might lead him. In a short while he came to a small crossing over a slow-flowing stream. The stream was about six feet wide. Waldo loved water, and all that lived in it. He was instantly drawn to it. He dropped to the ground to see what might be swimming beneath the water. He used his hands to create shade, so that he could see through the reflections from the sky above on the water's surface. Waldo peered intently into the depths of the stream beneath. Deep beneath the surface of the water, he could see the pebbled bottom about two metres down.

There was a dense school of silver fish with elongated bodies, swimming calmly in the water. They glistened as their silver scales turned to the sun, and reflected the sunlight back to the waters surface. The stream's bottom was a dull golden colour as it was lit up by the bright sunlight above. It was covered in small dark-brown rocks that had been smoothed round by the years of water flowing over them. They were about the size of a hand, and there were numerous lush dark-green water plants swaying in the waters flow. Reaching out his hand, Waldo touched the water. It felt cool, about eighteen degrees he thought. He cupped some of the water in his hands, and smelt it. It smelt good, so he tasted a small amount. Deciding it was safe to drink, and he drank his fill.

The sun was almost straight up now. "Midday," Waldo thought, as he looked at his watch. His watch indicated it was 8:30am. "Mmm, that's strange," he thought to himself, "Must be in a different time zone," so he set the second-time zone on his watch to 12:00pm. The sun was getting hotter and with the warm air, Waldo felt the urge to swim. He stripped off his clothes and eased into the water. When he got in, the water felt cold, so he swam upstream to warm his body up. He swam about twenty metres. There the stream meandered, and a corner formed a large hole that had been etched away by the many years of flowing water. The hole was much deeper. Waldo took a large breath, and duck dived. He took a closer look at the stream's pebbled bed. It was covered in water plants and smooth round stones. Something was shining in the sun. His breath was running low, so he took one final glance, noted its position, and went up for air. Taking another deep breath he dived down again. Lying between the pebbles, there was a round silver case. It glistened as it reflected the sun from the stream's floor. Waldo reached out and picked it up. He then swam to the surface.

Waldo swam to the waters edge and placed the silver case on the grassy bank. He dived under the water again several more times, as he searched the entire stream bed for more treasures, but there was nothing more to be found. Waldo pulled himself up onto the grassy bank, found his clothes and after drying a short while in the warm sun, got dressed. He settled down by the bridge over the stream and studied the silver case very carefully. It looked like it was made of pure silver. It is certainly heavy enough to be he thought. Waldo weighed it in his hand. It was circular, about half the size of the palm of his hand, and elaborately embossed. It had a silver dragon with its body wrapped around a crescent moon engraved on it. Its large folded wings extended out from the outer arch of the crescent moon, and its tail extended from the tip of the crescent's bottom right around to form a circle with the upper tip of the crescent. The dragon's body was intricately engraved with silver scales, and the dragon's golden eyes had thin black slits as pupils.

There was a small button on the front of the delicately hinged case. Waldo pressed the button and the case sprung open. Inside the case was perfectly dry, and lying inside its polished silver lining was the most magnificently etched ivory amulet. Waldo picked up the amulet in his hand and studied it closely. It was of the same design as the picture on the outside of the case, with the dragon wrapped around the curve of a crescent moon. It was attached to a shining solid silver linked chain. The amulet was magnificently crafted with fine scales carved on both sides of the dragon's body, intricate and beautiful in its carved detail.

Inside the lid of the amulet's case, Waldo noticed an inscription. It was in a foreign language, so he couldn't read what it said. If only Waldo could have read what is said, he would have known that it contained a very important warning:

"WARNING!! Whoever dares to wear the sign of the Maligrandé shall survive only if, they are pure of heart and soul, and born of earth and water, in the year of the dragon. For only a truly righteous one can receive the gifts from The Source of Life and live. For only the one who is all of these things will live, and be known to all, as the mighty one, who is—The Maligrandé!"

On studying the amulet very carefully, Waldo could see that this was no ordinary artefact, and he supposed it must be extremely valuable. He wondered whose it might have been. He hung the amulet around his neck and then studied it admiringly. He picked up the silver case, closed it, and put it in his pocket. Many before Waldo had done exactly the same thing. They had also been overwhelmed by their good luck. Indeed, it was a precious find, and Waldo could hardly stop smiling he was so happy. Waldo of course had no idea, that all who had worn the amulet before him, had on the next rising of the full moon— perished!

Waldo continued his journey. He was feeling relaxed and content. He continued the journey down the dirt path as instructed by the Black Rabbit, and it wasn't long before he was through the clearing, and into the tall forest trees at the other side. The path led up and down small undulating hills, and around twists and turns, as it meandered through the forest floor. After a time Waldo found himself looking across the top of a deep valley. It was cleared at the bottom where it was covered in flat green grass. In the valley, Waldo could see a small cottage. A single stream of smoke rose straight up into the still air from the chimney in the rear.

The dirt path wound its way down the hill. In fact, it went right by the cottage situated in the valley at the bottom. Waldo's heart raced when he saw an elderly man with a staff. The aged man was walking toward the house. He wobbled from side to side as he walked, as if he was carrying a war wound in one leg. His shoulders were slightly hunched, as if he was carrying a heavy pack, which he wasn't, and he was wearing an old navy blue air force cap.

Even from the top of the hill, Waldo recognised that very distinctive walk. It was the very familiar waddle of his old friend Mr. Campbell, who used to live just down the road from Waldo. When Waldo was about twelve years old, in the school holidays, he would wave and say hi to Mr. Campbell every day. The old man would walk past Waldo's house, and then to the end of the red gravel road, to pick up his mail. Mr. Campbell didn't use a post office box like everyone else in the street. Instead, he used an old drum nailed on top of a post, at the corner of the main road, that the post run included.

Sometimes during the school holidays when Waldo got lonely, he would wander over to Mr. Campbell's house. Waldo always made his way to the back door, where there was always a small tomahawk lying on a bench. Mr. Campbell used the tomahawk to split kindling for his fire. Waldo would go to the back door, and thump the blunt end of the tomahawk on the splitting block. Upon hearing the knock, Mr. Campbell would come out through his kitchen's fly-wire screen-door. Waldo and Mr. Campbell would stand around and chat, until eventually, they would decide it was time to potter off and do something else.

Mr. Campbell had left the house next door to Waldo's some time ago. Waldo had heard nothing of him since. He was an old man, with an oval-shaped Gommer Pile looking face. He even had a Gommer Pile big toothy smile. His face was much older now, and his wrinkle lines were deep. Mr. Campbell had bright blue eyes. He was pretty much completely bald, which is why he always wore a blue air force cap on his head. It had never occurred to Waldo before, but maybe he was an ex-air force man, and maybe he was shot in the leg, during World War II.

In any case, it mattered not, for Mr. Campbell was one of those old folks you just couldn't get enough of. The funny thing was, he never talked that much, but when he did he was kind and uncomplicated. Waldo liked him a lot, and wished he hadn't gone away. Waldo had assumed, after all these years, that Mr. Campbell had died. How he could have possibly turned up here, was as mysterious as the place itself.

In his excitement, Waldo hurled himself down the path, which wound through the tall timbers to the valley floor. He was outside of Mr. Campbell's cottage in around fifteen minutes. He gathered his breath, and ran to the back door. Sure enough, there was a pile of firewood and a small tomahawk and a chopping block there. Waldo picked up the tomahawk and hit it hard on the block two times, so that it made sufficient noise for Mr. Campbell to hear. There was a stirring from behind the solid oak door. Finally, it swung inward and there stood the old man whom Waldo had seen from the top of the hill. Waldo enquired, "Mr. Campbell is that you?" The old man peered out of the door and seeing the lad standing there hobbled out. "Waldo Middins, is that you? Well look at you my boy. My, you have grown to be quite a strapping young man. Well, I never. Come in lad, come in."

So as it turned out, Waldo had indeed found his long-lost friend, and as puzzling as it all was he was very glad to see him again. Mr. Campbell was about to eat lunch, so he invited Waldo to join him. Whilst they ate the stew Mr. Campbell had cooked, and drank tea, they talked. Waldo explained how he had chased the Black Rabbit and fallen through the ring of toadstools. Strangely, Mr Campbell didn't know anything about the toadstools, and he didn't really have any idea of how or when he had moved here. In fact, as far as he could recall, he must have moved there some time ago, but as his memory was failing him, he couldn't really say when or how. Nevertheless, Mr. Campbell thought that this was a fine place to live. Since moving here, his arthritis did not give him any trouble whatsoever.

Waldo enquired as to the name of this place, but Mr. Campbell didn't have a name for it. He asked where the path he was following led to, and did he know anything about the Great Book of Knowledge, but alas Mr. Campbell knew nothing of either of these things. Waldo pulled the silver case from his pocket, and he asked Mr. Campbell if he had ever seen anything like it. Mr. Campbell studied it hard. He thought it looked like it had something to do with a Moon Dragon, but he had no knowledge of it. Waldo told Mr. Campbell, he wanted him to keep the case, as a memento. Mr. Campbell took the sliver case, and placed it on his mantle piece beside an old antique clock. He said whenever he saw it, he would think of Waldo, and that he was very grateful. As he did so, the clock struck one. Waldo looked at his watch. It read twelve forty-five pm, so he set it to the time on Mr. Campbell's clock.

Waldo showed Mr. Campbell the amulet as it hung around his neck. At one-point Waldo tried, but strangely he couldn't seem to manage to remove it. Unperturbed, Waldo moved on and started explaining his search for a crystal that could transport people. Mr. Campbell just looked sad. He didn't know how he could help Waldo, and he didn't want Waldo to leave either. Waldo decided to stop asking questions, that Mr. Campbell clearly didn't know how to answer. After they had chatted for some time, Waldo finally insisted, that it was time for him to go. So Mr. Campbell packed him a kaki backpack of supplies, including a sleeping bag, a small tent, some matches, utensils, and enough food and water to last a few days. The two old friends bid each other good day, and Waldo set off on his journey again. Waldo looked at his watch. It was two in the afternoon.

The path led across the long valley floor, and then up across the mountain, that surrounded it on the other side. The mountain was steep, and it was hard going. Waldo stopped to rest every thirty minutes or so. After several hours, Waldo finally made it to the top of the mountain. He surveyed the view for a short while, and then started heading down the other side. After two more hours of walking, the light started to fade. It became clear to Waldo, that night would soon be here. He found a small flat clearing, pitched the tent, and made his bed. He gathered some stones, made a circle with them, gathered some wood, and lit a fire for the night.

Waldo heated some baked beans, and ate them straight from the can with a bun. He boiled some water in the small billy from his pack, and made some black tea to drink. As he ate his dinner, the noises from the forest in the daytime faded, and became silent. The sun had now gone down, and the sky was becoming dark. As the sky blackened, stars appeared against the night sky. It wasn't long before it was dotted all over with sparkling stars. Waldo watched the stars as they twinkled at him. He thought how different the constellations were from the night skies back home. It was then that the moon moved into view. It was the biggest moon he had ever seen. It felt so close. He tried to reach out and touch it with his hand. The moon light lit the entire forest floor. It was, in fact, a full moon . . .

Waldo huddled by the fire to keep warm. He thought long and hard about what had happened to him that day. His thoughts made him sad, and he was overcome with emotion, as he thought about how he may never get back home. For the first time in a long time, he prayed. Suddenly, a fresh breeze shook the tree tops. It sent cold shivers down Waldo's spine. The fire flickered as the flames fought the icy fingers of the cool breeze. Waldo knew this heralded a cold change. As he looked into the distant sky, he noticed the stars had disappeared behind the black curtain that was moving across the sky. There was nothing left but a thick blackness. A cold front was moving in fast. It looked and felt like it would rain very soon.

Waldo remembered how he loved to snuggle up in his warm bed at home. He recalled how his warm snug toes felt so good all wrapped up in his blankets. He remembered how much he loved to listen to the rain fall on the tin roof. Already the air had become quite cold. Waldo hurried to his tent. He wanted to be warm and snug by the time the rain came, so he crawled into the tent, snuggled up in the sleeping bag and lay on his back listening. Occasionally, he could hear the wind racing through the treetops in large swooshes and whirls.

The leaves of the trees rattled against each other, wooshing and wailing in the wind. After about half an hour passed, Waldo could hear the dull sporadic thud of very large raindrops falling on leaves and ground. At first, the rain started falling very slowly with great gaps between drops, but then as the clouds moved overhead and blackened the forest by blocking out the moon, the rain became steady. In a strange way Waldo felt safe and at peace, just as if he was on a camping trip with his family in the bush back home. Waldo thought to himself, "If I should die tonight, I would die content."

Waldo had little idea of the irony of his thoughts. As the full moon began its night's journey, Waldo snug in his bed felt toasty and warm. He felt safe, very safe. The rain would keep the creeping and crawling creatures of the night inside their holes, and the icy winds would keep any other animals from venturing outside of their warm snug hollows, burrows and caves, as well. Apart from the unlikely event of a wild storm sending branches crashing to the ground, and thunder and lightning striking the trees or his tent, he could be confident he was going to be safe and warm and dry.

Waldo loved the sound of the rain on the tent roof. It was so peaceful. Waldo savoured the sound of the rain as he fought off the great tiredness that overcame him. It was a very physical day for him, and despite his best efforts, Waldo soon fell fast asleep. As Waldo slept soundly and ever so deeply, the night continued on its journey. It extinguished Waldo's fire, and as Waldo slept, the forest around him was consumed by cleansing rain. The cold wind howled through the tree tops, as the thick black darkness of storm clouds rolled in overhead.

Several hours passed. Waldo was in such a warm deep sleep that he didn't even hear the great whoosh, whooshing sound of giant wings that buffeted his tent. Nor did he hear the weighty thud that sounded a short distance away, or the heavy breathing sounds that followed. There was a snort from nostrils larger than that of a horse sniffing the air. The storm had subsided, at least, for the moment, and the air was still. The rain stopped.

The amulet around Waldo's neck began to glow. The beast moved closer, and as it did the amulet glowed even more. It shone a dazzling white as it sent streams of light radiating upward through the roof of the tent. The ground vibrated from the weight of the massive beast as it dragged its weighty body closer. It edged closer and closer until it was right up beside, and touching the tent walls. The amulet was glowing so brightly now that it was getting warm. The brighter the amulet glowed the hotter and hotter it became. It got so hot that it started to burn Waldo's skin. Waldo woke up to the smell of burning flesh—his burning flesh!

Suddenly, Waldo was wide-awake. He screamed aloud with the intense pain! He tried to pull the amulet from his neck, but it burnt his hands. He couldn't get it off. It just kept burning into his skin where it had been resting on his chest, just below the base of his neck. As the light from the amulet flooded the tent with its shining white aura, Waldo struggled to get out of his sleeping bag. He struggled towards the tent door when he heard a loud snort outside, and a thud that made the ground shake. Waldo stiffened in horror. He dared not go out. He fell backward with the excruciating pain—it was getting worse!

The amulet's light shone whiter, and then even brighter, until the entire tent glowed a shining white. The pain worsened, and then it got even worse. Waldo felt his whole-body stiffen as it began to levitate, and he rose horizontally into the air. He couldn't move his arms or legs anymore. His skin became so hot that he could see steam rising from it, and he could feel pressure building up inside of him under his skin. His skin started to bubble from beneath. Waldo was sure, that the bubbles bubbling underneath his skin, would burst at any moment. It was like watching sulphur bubbling in a steaming mud pool.

The bubbles under his skin hastened in their effervescence. Waldo's eyes and mouth were wide open with the horror of it. He was confused and in great pain. He could do nothing but watch the bubbles all over the underside of his skin, form and disappear. As if this wasn't bad enough, his entire body was overcome with uncontrollable convulsions, and the pain became so intense inside his head that his brain felt like it would explode. Waldo's heart began to beat so hard and rapidly in his chest, that he could hear it pounding, faster and faster, louder and louder.

With every beat, his chest expanded and contracted, so that it was plain to see his hearts rapid pumping on the outer-side of his skin. It left mounds on the outside as it pumped harder and harder. In his last conscious moments, Waldo wished he would die quickly. His life flashed before his eyes. The whole time, he was screaming in excruciating agony.

All went suddenly silent. Waldo's screams stopped as his body went limp. Every cell in his body had been separated and was now swirling around in a melting pot of his own hot flesh and blood. It boiled within him, bubbles bubbling everywhere, engulfing his entire body beneath his skin; such was the painful horror that had befallen Waldo. It was the excruciating journey of death that so many before him had followed, and perished. It was a journey no one had ever survived.

In the silence, Waldo's body slowly returned to the ground, and the amulet's glow began to fade. After a few minutes of waiting, the beast tilted its head back so that it pointed skyward. It let out a huge roar, and flames leapt into the air for twenty meters. The forest all around was lit by the glow of its orange light.

The beast raised its large scaly wings and strummed the air. Its body lifted skyward, and as the whooshing sounds of its giant wings faded into the distance, there was nothing but silence. The amulet stopped glowing. Waldo's body lay outstretched on the ground inside the tent. He was lying on his back—lifeless! His eyes were closed. Wafts of burnt flesh and steam rose silently in the darkness. The rain started again.

In the morning, the clouds had cleared the sky, and the sun was shining brightly again. Its rays warmed the fresh washed earth, and there was an invigorating wet earthy smell of the forest after rain, lingering in the air. Steam rose from the drying leaves and grasses. As one does when one wakes from the most terrible of nightmares, Waldo's eyes opened in bewilderment and horror. He sat up with a start. He was alive!

Waldo fumbled for his shirt and trousers. He hurriedly put them on. He was shaking all over from his ordeal. For the second time in two days Waldo's heart raced fiercely with fear. He was dazed and confused. He could scarcely believe what had happened. He felt light-headed. He went pale. He could feel a rush of blood going from his head. He felt dizzy. Suddenly, he felt like he was about to throw up. He stood up and clambered out of the tent as fast as he could. Then he froze solid—he was terrified! There, standing right in front of him, with its head raised and lizard eyes glaring down at him, sat a massive silver-scaled dragon. Its scales dazzled Waldo's eyes as they reflected the sun's light. Its long snout and large nostrils were so close that with every breath, the dragon breathed warm air fell all over Waldo. He couldn't move. His voice was gone. He was frozen to the spot.

The dragon swung his head and placed it right up close to Waldo's. It looked at him intently in the eyes. The dragon's eyes were yellow with large black slits for pupils. Waldo dared not move. Waldo knew in that moment that last night was, in fact, very real! He was still hoping it was all a bad dream, but now he knew. It was not a dream. Waldo was terrified by the dragon baring down on him. He thought he would be devoured. He felt the blood rushing from his head as he turned a ghostly white.

His life flashed before his eyes once more. Waldo passed out and fell unconscious to the ground. It was all too much for him to bear.

When Waldo came too, he was snuggled up in the front legs of the dragon. The dragon was now lying down with its belly on the ground. Its front legs were folded. It had wrapped its neck and head around so that it formed a soft bed for Waldo to recover in. Waldo was resting snugly in the warmth made by the dragon's neck and its front leg. When he awoke, nearly an hour had passed by. Waldo could feel the warm breath of the dragon. Its scales were soft and smooth, yet tough enough to serve as extremely strong armour.

Waldo thought through his situation for a short time. He decided that he no longer should be afraid of the dragon. After all he was still ALIVE! It was clear now, that the dragon meant him no harm, for if it did, it would have eaten him already. Waldo stood up slowly. He took a few paces backward so he could get a good look at the dragon. The dragon raised its head and looked at him in pure delight.

"H-He-Hello," said Waldo gingerly.

"Don't be afraid," said the dragon in a soft deep tone that was so low, everything vibrated.

"Are you a dragon?" asked Waldo.

"I am the Moon Dragon," replied the dragon. The dragon asked in a soothing, enquiring voice, "So tell me . . . what is your name?"

"My name is Waldo," Waldo replied.

"Why are you here?" Waldo asked.

"Oh I came in hope that finally after so many millions of years that my search may end . . . and last night—finally, my search did end young Waldo."

Waldo questioned, "Search for what?"

"I have been searching for The Maligrandé," replied the dragon

Waldo enquired, "The Maligrandé?"

"Yes," said the dragon, "The Maligrandé is one pure of heart and soul, born of air and water, for only one truly righteous can receive the gifts of the Source of Life. Last night your heart and soul were confronted by the ultimate test of life and death. This was because you wore the Maligrandé's amulet around your neck. By doing so, you offered yourself for testing by the ancient powers that forged the gifts from the Source of Life itself into the amulet."

Waldo reached down his shirt. He grasped the amulet still hanging around his neck and pulled it out. As he clasped it in his hand, it disintegrated into a fine white dust. The powder formed in the air into a swarm of white sparkling particles. Each dust grain rose up and took on a life of its own. Together the dust swirled and swarmed. The small white glistening grains hovered just above Waldo's head, and then like bees the swarm zoomed off into the sky above. Waldo and the dragon watched, as it disappeared over the distant hills beyond.

Waldo exclaimed, "It's gone!"

"Look under your shirt Waldo," said the dragon.

Waldo unbuttoned his shirt to see what the dragon was wanting him to see. On his chest where the Ivory Amulet had burnt into his skin, he now had a raised scar. It was in the shape of the dragon wrapped around the crescent moon. Every intricate detail on the amulet was now in his scar. The scar was completely healed. Waldo couldn't believe it. He remembered the amulet burning into his chest last night. He remembered the pain he had suffered. Strangely now, there was no pain at all.

The dragon continued to explain, "Last night the power of the full moon and my presence combined with the powers within the amulet, to release the gifts that the Source of Life had sealed within it. Your body was transformed. The process prepared your body Waldo, so that you might be able to receive what the Source of Life was about to offer you. You see Waldo, the amulet and I were both created from the same essence in the universe. Like blood brothers, when we are together, we complete the Source of Life. Last night, the gifts sealed within the amulet were offered to you. No wearer of the amulet has ever been able to receive the gifts sealed within the amulet before Waldo. They all died, thousands of them over the ages. That is, until you Waldo."

Waldo exclaimed, "I thought I was going to die!"

The dragon continued. "Yes Waldo, and thousands who have dared to wear the amulet have died before you, however, you survived Waldo," said the dragon with a grin.

Waldo asked, "Why did the others die?"

"Unfortunately if the wearer is unable to receive the Source of Life's gifts, the amulet has no choice but to re-absorb the gifts back into itself. This process creates immense energy. It produces white heat in the reverse process, that is so intense, it is fatal to the wearer. They have all been cremated by the heat. All that remains of them is ash now."

Waldo enquired, "So how did I survive?"

"Well Waldo, when the amulet glows, it re-structures the cells in the wearer's body. This enables the body to be prepared so it can receive the powerful gifts being transferred. This was a great test of your inner soul, your strength, your character, your righteousness, and therefore, your capacity to be able to stay true to the world of all things good. Once you have received the gifts from the Source of Life, you and I henceforth, complete the circle within the Source of Life. You passed that test Waldo, and in doing so the process of transferring from the amulet to you burnt that scar onto your chest. It is the mark of the Maligrandé Waldo. Whoever sees this mark, will know, that you are truly the one and only—The Maligrandé," explained the dragon.

Waldo questioned some more, "But how and why me?"

"Your birth is of earth and water, in the year of the dragon, and only these birth elements can combine with the fire and air of the Moon Dragon to complete the Source of Life. From now on, Waldo, you and I, will be as one, and when we are together, the Source of Life will be complete and strong."

Waldo asked, "So what are the gifts I have been given?"

"In time, you will discover what the gifts are Waldo. I cannot tell you what they are, as these are yours alone to discover. The gifts will not reveal themselves until you are ready for them Waldo, but as you need them, rest assured, they will be revealed to you," explained the dragon knowingly.

Waldo confirmed, "So I am The Maligrandé . . ."

"Yes," said the dragon. "I have been sending envoys to seek out those born of earth and water for the past millennium. I have sent them to the outer reaches of space seeking those born of that constellation, so that they might be tested to see if they were, in fact, The Maligrandé. Only one, truly pure of heart and soul, who is truly at one with the earth and water, and whose soul is also as pure in thought of all things good, could ever be trusted with such gifts, hence only one such as this could ever pass the test."

Waldo questioned, "Did you say outer reaches?"

"Yes all of them," said the Dragon, "There are many. This world is a channel for the entire universe. It is the white light that keeps the outer worlds in balance. Everything comes through here sooner or later Waldo—lost civilisations, knowledge, technology, thoughts, good and evil—they are all here, and from here anything is possible."

Waldo asked, "So what do they call this world?"

"This world is called Annulus, Waldo. It is the middle of all creation, where it never begins and never ends," replied the dragon.

Waldo thought for a minute and then asked, "So is this heaven?"

"No Waldo, but even the answers to these things can be found here. Seek and you shall find them."

Waldo enquired, "So what's next then?"

"I will take you to the City of Gold," said the dragon. "There you must retrieve the Great Book of Knowledge, Waldo. I cannot enter the City of Gold, for the City of Gold is a Sun City, and I am a Moon Dragon. In the City of Gold, there are dark forces at work, so you must be careful Waldo. You can trust no one. The Great Book was stolen by a truly evil man. He is too evil, as you are too good. He is known as the Salimandé, and you will need to be very careful in your quest for the Great Book, as he will guard it with all of his evilness, and his evilness is great.

He is your extreme opposite in the universe. You two are diametrically opposed to each other. He also has powerful gifts, but his source grows from evilness and death. He surrounds himself with black-hearted evil people. He gains his strength from the sun, whereas your source grows from goodness and life. You will surround yourself with love, and you gain your strength from the moon. You are now re-born of the silvery moon, and from it stems love, romance, and the light in all things good. The Salimandé is born of the golden sun. He uses fire, hate, and the greed instilled in all mankind, to spread evilness into the world."

The dragon went on to explain, "The City of Gold is not heavily guarded, as none who enters ever leaves. Whenever anyone enters the City of Gold, they are held captive there by the black thoughts they have within themselves. Only one truly pure of heart can go there and leave. Nevertheless, Waldo, you must go there and retrieve the Great Book. Once we have it, we will quickly return it to its rightful place. It will restore peace and harmony to the land, and its people will rejoice in its return.

This will be a very dangerous quest Waldo. If you are captured by the Salimandé, he will want to destroy you. You must never forget Waldo. You are The Maligrandé, and the Source of Evil will always seek to be rid of you. Once the Salimandé knows of your existence, he will stop at nothing to remove the balance of good, that through you, has now been restored. This is the beginning of your new life as the Maligrandé, Waldo, and with this new life comes great responsibility in the call to the service of good. Soon you will discover what this truly means, and when you discover what you as the Maligrandé must do, you may find that much more may be asked of you than you can possibly be ready to give, however, you alone are capable of meeting this responsibility. For you are the chosen one."

"I am not sure I want to do this," said Waldo with some reluctance.

The dragon exclaimed, "You must!"

"Much is at stake. This is your destiny now Waldo. You are the one and only—The Maligrandé."

"What does Maligrandé mean anyway?" questioned Waldo.

"It means the beholder of the Source of Life," said the dragon.

"Mmm—Makes sense," Waldo responded with a nod.

Waldo lit a fire. He thought deeply about what the dragon had said. He heated up some more food out of the pack that Mr. Campbell had given him. He ate it whilst the dragon watched patiently. He asked the dragon if he wanted some of his food, but the dragon said he didn't need to eat. He explained he got his energy from the moon. After some time had passed, Waldo said, "You know Moon Dragon is an awfully long name."

"Well actually, I have never been given a proper name," the dragon replied.

Mmm thought Waldo, "Then I shall give you a name."

The dragon exclaimed excitedly, "Really!"

"Yes," said Waldo. "From this point on you, Moon Dragon of Annulus, shall be known as . . . let me think . . . . how about . . . Miadrag?"

"Mmm," said the dragon, "Miadrag Moon Dragon, Miadrag and Waldo . . . has a nice ring to it doesn't it? Yes indeed— Miadrag it shall be," confirmed the dragon happily.

Miadrag and Waldo laughed and chatted as Miadrag watched Waldo pack the backpack with all of his things. At last, Waldo flung the backpack on his back and started walking down the path.

Miadrag questioned, "Where are you going Waldo?"

"To find the Great Book of course" said Waldo, quite matter of fact.

The dragon responded, "Jump on Waldo . . . why walk . . . when we can FLY!"

Waldo after a few failed attempts, managed to fix himself fast between Miadrag's shoulders with his arms wrapped around Miadrag's neck. "Hold on tight Waldo, here we go." Miadrag stood up. His giant wings beat the air. His great bulk rose slowly into the sky, and they were off.

Journey to the City of Gold

lying on the dragon's back, as it turned out, actually wasn't that hard. The ride was surprisingly smooth. In no time at all, Waldo and Miadrag were flying high above the ground below. They could see a magnificent blue mountain range in the distance, green valleys and forests beneath them, and a deep wide river that snaked its way though the land as far as the eye could see.

From time to time, they would fly over small villages. They could see people working in the fields surrounding the villages. Waldo watched the villagers using horses to draw their carts, and he noted that the clothes they were wearing looked like they were straight out of an old-time pioneer movie. Waldo could see the odd wagon trail, but there were no other man-made roads to speak of. The people around seemed quite used to the dragon, as they were clearly not afraid of it. Some of the villagers even stopped what they were doing to wave to the dragon. Children would sometimes run after the dragon, but they would barely get anywhere at all, before they were left far behind.

Waldo was enjoying the ride. They flew effortlessly through the sky. The air was warm. It felt good as it blew his hair backward from his face. From time to time, Miadrag would fly above the clouds. Waldo had never seen clouds at such close range before, and he was amused by the fact that they were fluffy on the top, as well as on the bottom. Waldo enjoyed the bright blue sky, and the warm sun shining above the clouds. By the end of each day, Waldo grew very tired, so at night they would stop and rest. Waldo slept in his tent, as the dragon settled down close by, to watch over him.

For the first time in thousands of years, Miadrag felt content and complete. He couldn't remember any other time, that he had felt this good. As the moon rose each night, the dragon's scales would shine in the moonlight, and the moon's energy would replenish him as he bathed in its light. The dragon loved it when the moon rose, and he mused at Waldo's sleeping body levitating. The scar on his chest was shinning white, as it too drew energy from the moon. Its light was so bright, that it shone straight through the sides of Waldo's tent. The dragon knew that with every sleep, Waldo would grow stronger. The Source of Life was making small chemical adjustments in his body. As these new chemicals reacted with the other chemicals in his body, new cells would form, and in time, Waldo's gifts would be complete.

In the mornings, Waldo would wake up feeling rested and strong. In fact, he couldn't remember when he had ever felt better. His dreams were happy dreams. He dreamt of the village people living their contented lives, and of him on the dragon's back, flying through the clear skies. Whenever Waldo saw the moon shinning, an inner peace would overwhelm him, and he would feel at one with the world. From time to time, he tried to imagine what the City of Gold would look like. Miadrag had warned him that there was great danger there. So as Waldo finished packing his backpack, he asked, "Miadrag . . . what is the City of Gold like?"

"It shines like the sun Waldo. When you see it from a distance it is like the setting sun shedding golden light far across the land, as if the sun itself is sinking beneath the distant horizon."

Waldo enquired, "Who built it?"

"The Mayans built it thousands of years ago, before they discovered another world which they thought was their after world, and moved on. The city draws its energy from the sun, and it shines both night and day. Strange folk the Mayans, for such an advanced civilisation, they never seemed to be able to work out their true destiny . . . oh well," Miadrag sighed.

"Who lives there now?" asked Waldo.

"Evil, Waldo. The City of Gold draws to it every living thing that ever existed that is vain, greedy and black-hearted. Evil can't help itself. It has to go there. Now it is a city of the damned Waldo."

Waldo questioned, "But everyone I've seen seems so happy and content?"

"People are happy and content here Waldo. That's because, when evil enters this world, it is immediately drawn to the City of Gold. Once there, it becomes trapped there forever. You see Waldo, to dark souls, the city is a great source of riches. It feeds their greed so much, that they can never bear to leave it. They spend all their time there, stealing and oppressing each other."

"I don't want to go there," replied Waldo.

"Me neither," said the dragon, "but go there we must."

"Won't I be conspicuous?" Waldo asked.

"Everyone who enters through the great gates of the City of Gold is given a black robe with a hood. This is what they all wear. They do this so they can disguise themselves from each other. You won't stand out Waldo . . . no . . . you will look just like the rest of them."

Waldo sat quietly, and thought through what Miadrag had told him. It all sounded plausible enough, except for one minor detail. Waldo asked, "So why hasn't anyone taken the Great Book back already?"

"Some have tried Waldo. They have gone there with intentions of taking back the Great Book, but to bring yourself inside the Sun City, is to open yourself to black thoughts, and the smallest of these black thoughts, even with good intentions, is more than enough to trap your soul in the Sun City forever. You see the Sun City magnifies all evil thoughts, and those that have entered the city have lost their will to leave it."

"Has anyone ever returned?" questioned Waldo.

"Eh—no," replied Miadrag.

Waldo exclaimed, "Well how do you expect me too!"

"You are the Maligrandé Waldo."

"Some comfort that is," replied Waldo with a humph.

"Have faith in yourself Waldo. You will be fine," said Miadrag reassuringly.

"How long before we get there?" asked Waldo.

"Soon Waldo, soon," replied the dragon with a smile.

At that moment, there was the thunder of horse hooves galloping fast towards them. The dragon exclaimed, "Quick Waldo, jump on!" Waldo leapt onto the dragon's back. Miadrag flew into the air at such speed that Waldo could barely hold on. From the air, Waldo could see an army on horse back. They were very heavily armed. Their armour glistened in the sun. At the sight of the dragon, they halted abruptly, their horses rearing into the air, with the sudden pull on the bits in their mouths.

This was a bloodthirsty lot if ever Waldo had seen one. Waldo watched as they reached for their bows and arrows. They pointed the arrows skyward. Suddenly, the sky was filled with arrows. Some of the arrows hit Miadrag, but they simply bounced off his tough scales. Then it happened. As Miadrag veered left, and flew broadside to the bloodthirsty hoard, one of the hundreds of arrows fired into the air hit Waldo behind his left shoulder. The pain was excruciating. Waldo looked down. There was blood everywhere. The arrows blackened point had pierced straight-through Waldo's body. It was now sticking out of his chest. Waldo screamed, "I'm hit Miadrag!" Waldo held on as tight as he could, but his body was going into shock. He was feeling weaker and giddier with every breath. Miadrag flew away as fast as he could, to safety. The army let out a great roar at the dragon's retreat. It resumed its charge, heading off in the direction of the City of Gold.

Miadrag could feel Waldo's grip loosening, so he hastily found a village. It was some distance away, but it was in the opposite direction to the advancing army, so it would be safe enough there. Miadrag landed. The village was in partial ruins. The advancing army was destroying everything within its reach. Fortunately, the villagers received a timely warning of the army's blood seeking advance. They had just enough time to scramble to their underground hides, where they hid from the oppressors until they were gone. Many of the huts they lived in were on fire. When the dragon landed, the villagers were coming out from hiding, so they could extinguish the fires. On seeing Waldo struggling to stay on the dragon's back, they raced to his aid.

Within seconds of landing, Waldo collapsed. He couldn't hold on any longer. He slipped into unconsciousness and slid from Miadrag's back, and down his side. The villagers quickly rushed to catch Waldo as he fell. They carefully picked him up, and hurriedly carried him to one of their spare huts. The dragon settled outside of the hut and waited. The villagers broke the arrow and removed it. The arrow had just missed Waldo's heart. Blood was flowing freely. They placed a poultice on the wound, and wrapped it tightly. The bleeding slowed, but it didn't stop for some time after. Waldo lost a great deal of blood. He would remain weak and unconscious until his body could replenish it.

The villagers told the dragon how lucky Waldo had been, and that his wounds were very serious, but they expected he would make a full recovery over time. They told the dragon that Waldo would need plenty of rest. It would be several months before Waldo's wound would heal enough for him to travel again. The dragon thanked the villagers for their kindness, and he told them how grateful he was for their help.

Miadrag knew that if he remained in the village, it would attract too much attention to it. He told the villagers that he must go, but he would be protecting the village from the air in case another army happened to come their way. The villagers were grateful to the dragon, as they waved good bye, they comforted him. They reassured Miadrag that they would take good care of Waldo. The dragon raised his giant wings, and flew off.

Later, that afternoon, Waldo broke into semi-consciousness. His shoulder was throbbing with acute pain. It sent stabbing jolts through his shoulder and chest, every time he tried to move. His head was a daze, and he could barely recall what had happened. He was given something to drink. It tasted bad, but it did ease his pain. It made him feel even sleepier.

As he fell asleep, he caught a glimpse of the beautiful young woman who had been tending to his wounds. Her look was gentle and kind, and her eyes expressed considerable concern for him. She was sitting beside him on the bed holding the cup that he had been drinking from. He couldn't help but be consumed by her tremendous beauty. She had soft brown eyes, long crinkly black hair, and the most beautifully straight white teeth. When she smiled, her smile lit up the room. Despite his every effort to remain awake, Waldo fell into a deep sleep.

When night fell, the dragon returned. He watched over Waldo's hut as the young woman attended Waldo. The dragon couldn't help but notice how wonderfully caring she was, as she attended Waldo's wound. She was so gentle, and when she looked at Waldo with her soft brown eyes, her face was overcome with her deep concern for him. It was as if she could actually feel his pain. When she had finished attending to his wound, she left Waldo and the dragon, and returned to her family.

It was dark, and the moon was rising. As with every other night, as the moon rose, Waldo's body rose too. Ever so slowly it levitated into the air until it lay restfully a few feet above the bed. The blanket over him draped down. The scar on his chest was shining white under the blanket, and for the rest of the night as the moon shone, Waldo's body was healed and rejuvenated by the moon's energy and the Source of Life. At the same time, the Source of Life continued to make new types of cells, as it further developed Waldo's powerful gifts.

In the mornings, at the first hint of dawn, the dragon flew away. As the moon set, Waldo would stop levitating. He would ever so slowly sink back down to his bed again. It was some time after, as Waldo lay dreaming, that he was suddenly woken by a sharp pain in his chest. He opened his eyes with a flinch, only to find the woman of his dreams, just inches away from his face. He took a deep breath, so that he could smell her sweet scent.

The young woman was carefully trying to peel off his blood-stained bandages, in order to change them, and avoid the wound becoming infected. When Waldo flinched, she said, "Sorry Waldo. I was trying not to hurt you, but the bandage was stuck to your skin." Waldo could not help thinking how beautiful her voice was. "It's ok," said Waldo, as he sucked the pain in. The young woman noticed he was staring straight into her soft brown eyes. She smiled softly back at him. She blushed just a little, and continued to attend him.

As Waldo looked into her eyes, he had the irresistible urge to say, "You have me at a disadvantage as you know who I am, but I don't know who you are?"

She replied, "Macey . . . Macey Sanders. You were ever so lucky you know. A little to the right and you would have been killed by that arrow," she said. "You will have a nice scar, but nothing like the one you already have. How ever did you get a scar like that anyway?" asked Macey. Waldo's face looked lost. He struggled with what he might say, but before he could utter a single word, Macey said soothingly, "I'm sorry, I didn't mean to pry."

Waldo relieved from no longer being on the spot asked, "So how am I doing?" He tucked his chin in and tried to look down his nose at his wound. "You're doing just fine. In fact, I have never seen a wound heal so quickly. You should be up and around within a few weeks at this rate," Macey replied cheerfully. Macey finished changing Waldo's bandage, gathered the old dressings, and gave him the most beautiful smile as she left the room. Waldo didn't want her to go, so he tried moving as she left. He wanted to follow her, but the pain shot through his shoulder making him wish he hadn't tried to move at all. He fell back flat on his back. He had no wish to try moving again, any time soon.

In her absence, Waldo's thoughts soon returned to Macey. She was so beautiful he thought, and somehow, she made him feel complete when she was near. Every time he looked at her stunning beauty, his heart raced. Whenever she was near him, he felt an uneasiness in his stomach. He felt emotionally charged, and he could feel his heart pounding anxiously. At the same time, he felt nervous and uneasy. He wondered if she felt the same way. When he looked into her eyes, and she smiled at him, he was sure that she felt something. Waldo couldn't wait for her to come back, besides, he was starving. He didn't need to wait for long. It was but a few minutes later. Macey returned with some broth. Waldo sat up, but it was obvious that this hurt him quite a lot as he did. Macey sat down on the bed beside him and slowly spoon-fed Waldo the broth. It tasted really good.

Waldo savoured every moment of Macey's attention. He took advantage of these close moments to examine every curve of her perfect face. Her pale skin was flawless. She had soft lips. Her teeth were perfect, and her hair felt soft and beautiful, as it occasionally brushed against his face. Every time she smiled at him, or she urged him to try to take some more broth, he was overcome with feelings he found difficult to contain. After Macey had fed Waldo the broth, she took the empty bowl and left. Waldo felt sleepy as he settled back down to rest. The herbs in the broth soon took effect. He quickly fell fast asleep again. Macey came back and sat with Waldo as he slept. She couldn't help notice what a handsome young man he was. She had never seen such sparkling blue eyes, and the way that he looked at her so intently, made her feel as if she would melt at any moment.

Several hours passed before Waldo started to stir. Macey quickly ran out of the hut. She didn't want to be caught admiring how handsome he was, in case he might discover her feelings for him. She scuttled away, her heart racing. She was blushing quite a lot. Macey returned discreetly, five minutes later, after she had time to compose herself. She asked Waldo if he was hungry. He told her he was, so she promptly fetched him some cooked chicken and helped him sit up. Waldo's left arm still wasn't able to be used yet so he carefully ate the chicken with his right hand. Waldo happened to catch one of Macey's looks. He smiled back at her knowingly. Macey turned bright red, made a lame excuse that she had some chores to do, and ran flustered from the hut. Waldo chuckled and smiled. He thought to himself with some satisfaction . . . she most definitely has feelings for me.

When darkness fell, Miadrag returned again. He poked his head in the hut and enquired softly, "Waldo . . . are you alright?"

"Getting better," said Waldo with a flinch as he sat up to look at the dragon. "Where have you been?" asked Waldo.

"I've been keeping guard. I had to torch another army that was heading this way today," whispered Miadrag.

"Where are they coming from?" asked Waldo.

"They come from everywhere, but they are all heading to the same place. The City of Gold promises them their fortune. Unfortunately, until they find the City of Gold, they kill and maim all in their path," whispered Miadrag.

Miadrag enquired knowingly, "Has Macey been taking good care of you?"

"Sure," replied Waldo.

"She is a beautiful woman," said Miadrag teasingly.

Waldo asked, "Do you have someone Miadrag?"

"Oh, a long time ago," said Miadrag sadly.

Waldo replied, "So you know about love then?"

Miadrag exclaimed, "Why of course! I am a Moon Dragon, after all."

Waldo responded, "What's that got to do with it?"

"Have you ever heard of a romantic sun, or a sunlight walk by the beach? The moon is the source of all love Waldo, it is where romance fills the air, and lovers find each other."

Waldo thought for a long moment before he yawned, wished Miadrag a good night and fell fast asleep.

And so time passed. For the next few weeks Waldo and Macey laughed and talked a lot. They spent all of their free time together. They truly made each other happy, and they glowed with the love that grew between them. They simply grew fonder and fonder of each other, with every passing day. As they got to know each other better, they found that they had so many things in common. It was becoming very hard for them to be apart from each other, even for a short time.

As night came and Waldo slept, it was quite miraculous that Macey never caught Waldo levitating. Miadrag of course kept guard, and if anyone came at night, the dragon would wake Waldo, and he would sink to his bed, waking up just before they arrived. After two more weeks the levitations stopped. Though Waldo knew nothing of his sleeping flights, his body had now been completely transformed. The chemical changes required to affect his transformation, were finished.

Five weeks passed. Waldo's wound totally healed. He was now able to get up and walk around. Whilst his shoulder was still a bit sore, he needed to be careful with it, but so long as he didn't try to use it to do things too strenuous, it was fine. Macey was so happy that Waldo was up and about, as they could now take long walks together. Sometimes they would just sit in the middle of a field and stare into each other's eyes.

It was in one of these moments, on a perfectly sunny day in a field of bright yellow daisies, as Macey lay on the grass with Waldo lying on his side beside her, that Waldo rolled towards her, and every so slowly and deliberately, placed his lips on hers. Her lips were soft and moist. Waldo and Macey were both overwhelmed with their feelings, which exploded with a sudden and overwhelming passion. It was a wonderful moment, that would ignite a love that would bond their hearts together, for the rest of their lives.

From that point on, Macey and Waldo were a couple very much in love with each other, and they never let each other out of each other's sight for very long. The village folk smiled whenever they saw them together. They could see how much in love the two of them were. Miadrag was delighted too. His heart was filled with joy as he watched the two of them playing together as young lovers do. These were happy days indeed.

For Macey and Waldo, the next month was to be the happiest and most fulfilling time of their young lives. Waldo, was so caught up in his romancing of Macey, that he had completely forgotten about his past, and his troubles. One-day Macey asked him about his family, and Waldo suddenly recalled how he was trapped in this strange land, and so far he had found no way of returning home.

Waldo suddenly felt the weight of responsibility that had beseeched him. He couldn't help but remember that he was on a great quest to find the Great Book of Knowledge, held somewhere in the bowels of the terrible City of Gold. He shivered at the thought. He was so caught up in his love for Macey, that he had completely forgotten. The dragon had not reminded him either, nor had he urged him to move on in any way whatsoever. The fact was, that dragons have no need for haste, and Miadrag was so enjoying watching the love between Waldo, and Macey grow, that he didn't want to rush things in any case. Apart from that, the dragon knew that Waldo's gifts and shoulder weren't strong enough for him to fight off the

Salimandé, should he be discovered when he is in the City of Gold, and need to defend himself.

Macey sensing something was wrong asked, "Is everything okay Waldo?"

"Yes Macey . . . ," he replied, "I had just forgotten how I came to be here, and how long it had been."

Waldo told Macey all about his home and his family, and how he was trapped and needed to find a crystal so that he could one-day return. Macey feeling Waldo's sadness drew him close to her. She cuddled and ran her hands through his hair lovingly. Macey said she hoped, that whatever happened, they would always be together. Her candidness took Waldo a little by surprise. He was torn by the dilemma. It hadn't occurred to him until the very moment she said it. He pondered over the difficult decisions he would need to make in time. He was torn by his thoughts and his feelings. He knew at some point soon, he would need to choose which life, and indeed which world, he would make his own.

Suddenly, Macey jumped up and ran off giggling. Waldo chased her. When he caught her, he grabbed her, and they both fell to the ground laughing. Macey kissed Waldo, and then they kissed some more until they were so overcome by their love, they forgot about things that might be. They enjoyed the powerful moments that presented, there and then, in their overwhelming and powerful feelings for each other. They were so happy they were together now, it was easy to forget the harsh realities that lay before them. "Let's go to the river," said Macey, quickly standing up, as she tugged at Waldo's hand, "Come on," she urged. So Waldo got up. They walked together, hand-in-hand, to the river.

Waldo loved rivers. He loved to watch the under-currents rise from the deep dark-green waters as they swirled gently to the surface. He watched them slowly breaking away and dissipating, only to be followed a short time later by more rising currents. They were like the breath of the river, rising to the surface. He felt as if it was the rivers way of speaking with him in silent words that gave the river waters, life in itself. Waldo had often stared into the river's breath, trying to work out what it might be saying to him. It was so peaceful. He was often lost in his deep thoughts, mesmerised by the silence of the water in motion. He tried to make out what the sounds being spoken might be, as he studied the nature of each swirl.

The river was deep and wide. Small fish could be seen swimming in the shallows near the river's bank. They darted through the underwater plant leaves, in their search for food. There were willow trees that lined the banks. A warm breeze brushed the hanging fronds of the willows, ever so gently. It was a glorious day and so serene and peaceful by the river. There were ducks swimming close by. Macey loved to watch them. Waldo pointed out a large trout swimming close to the shore, and they both quietly lent forward to get a better look. They stood there in silence as the fish slowly swam by.

Suddenly, there was a whirring sound—crash! Waldo was knocked off his feet. He was hit by a black smoke billowing, red-hot fireball. He could see and smell the blackened burning flesh of his right shoulder. His shirt was blown to tatters by the fireball's impact. Macey screamed! Standing over her was a dark figure wearing a black hooded cloak. It had elongated red triangles that conjured images of evil and darkness, streaking down its painted face. It was completely black, with red flames bursting from its chin. They flared out across its cheeks. Its eyes glowed red. There was no doubting that this terrifying thing was most sinister. It seized Macey, clasped the glowing red crystal orb hanging around its neck, and in an instant, the two of them shimmered and were gone.

Waldo's heart sank as he struggled to get up. He was in shock, but it was the pain in his shoulder that stopped him, and he fell back. He must get up. "Get up! Get up!" Waldo kept shouting to himself, over and over. His emotions swelled with urgency . . . he must do something. Macey was in trouble.

Waldo placed his left hand over his wounded shoulder. He just wanted the pain to go away. As he thought of this, the scar on his chest glowed a bright shining white, and his hand glowed white too. His pain subsided. To his amazement, within the next few moments, his wound was completely healed. Waldo looked into his open cupped palms in amazement. He could heal himself! It was as if the fireball had never happened, well except for his tattered and charred shirt.

At first, Waldo was a bit stunned, and he just stood there for a moment . . . he just looked in bewilderment at his torn shirt. Then he got up, and ran. He ran as fast as he could, back to the village. He told the villagers what had happened to Macey, and they rallied around him, and comforted him. Macey's father told Waldo, "It was the Salimandé Waldo, the most evil being ever to exist. He will have taken her back to the City of Gold, and there is nothing we can do, for no-one has gone there, and returned."

Waldo exclaimed, "I must rescue her! Where is Miadrag? We must go at once!"

With that very thought, Miadrag was on his way to Waldo at high speed, for Miadrag had heard Waldo's cry for help, in his mind's eye. In fact, the dragon was able to listen to Waldo's thoughts for some time now. Within a matter of minutes, Waldo was leaping onto Miadrag's back, and they were in the air and travelling fast. Waldo could not believe his eyes, as Miadrag's wings were but a blur, as Miadrag hurtled them forward. Waldo held on tight, and he kept as low as he could to stop himself from being blown off the dragon's back by the rush of air that was caused by the great speed at which they flew. Within the hour, they could see on the distant horizon, the cold golden glow of the City of Gold. It was around three in the afternoon.

As the country raced by below, Waldo noticed that from time to time the fields beneath were littered with skeletons and decaying bodies. These were the remains of the bloody clashes of the armies that met on their respective journeys to the City of Gold. Even with these chance encounters, they would fight to the death, for to the victors would go the spoils of the City of Gold. That is what they thought anyway, and the fields below were littered with their black hearts. The closer they came to the City of Gold, the greater the carnage. The fields were filled with the overpowering smell of death, the product of their own greed.

A few hours later, the City of Gold came into full view. Above the city circled a large flying beast. From the distance, it was still nothing more than a large black blob. Waldo pointed in the general direction of the City of Gold and asked, "What's that flying over the city Miadrag?"

"That will be the Red Dragon Waldo. It spends all its time flying around the city and its outreaches, protecting the outside of the city from looters or other invaders. It is the Salimandé's Sun Dragon Waldo, just as I am the Maligrandé's Moon Dragon," replied Miadrag, "Not a particularly nice fellow I might add." Waldo pondered the implications of what Miadrag had said.

If the Salimandé has a Sun Dragon, and he, the Maligrandé has a Moon Dragon, it occurred to Waldo, that if he represented everything good, and the Salimandé represented everything that is evil, then maybe after all, this did truly mean that they were, in fact, the two opposing forces in the universe. The enormity of the position he was now in, suddenly became an overwhelming reality for Waldo.

As Waldo surveyed through these thoughts, a familiar voice joined in on his thought conversation.

"Ah I see you have discovered another gift Waldo," interrupted the voice of Miadrag. Waldo was stunned.

Waldo queried, "We can talk to each other without speaking?"

"Yes," replied Miadrag, "I guess your need to find me when you were back at the village, opened up your gift of telepathy, and you are right Waldo, you and I, the Salimandé and the Sun Dragon, do represent the equal and opposite opposing forces of good and evil in the universe."

Waldo questioned, "So that is what it truly means to be the Maligrandé?"

"Yes," replied Miadrag, "You are the universe's representative of all things good, and you must champion this cause, for all-kind."

"Wow!" thought Waldo.

"Wow indeed," said Miadrag.

The sun was starting to get lower in the sky now, and the City of Gold glowed an even darker and more intense shade of gold. In another hour, the sun would be down, and the city of gold would be in darkness. Miadrag had planned the timing of their arrival perfectly, as the evil forces within the city would be at their weakest after the sun had set. Miadrag and Waldo drew their energy from the moon, so they were at their strongest when the moon was in the sky. In the darkness, they would also be able to fly closer to the city without being detected.

Waldo opening up another thought conversation asked, "What will the Salimandé do with Macey?" "He will sacrifice her to the sun god Waldo. He will sacrifice her at noon tomorrow if we do not rescue her first. This is why we must hurry. The pagan rituals of the Mayan's are a favoured entertainment of the Salimandé, and he uses these rituals to twist the weak minds of his evil followers. He works them up into an evil frenzy, until they go crazy, chanting and blood-letting as they break into satanic dance. Then they seize their latest victims and plunge them into the areana. There they will be forced to fight to the death, or be slowly cremated by the Salimandé's fireballs. Better to die quickly by blade, than by the slow death by fireball that the Salimandé will bestow upon them." Waldo was revolted. It was hard to believe that he would soon be freely walking into such a den of unmentionable iniquity.

Battle of the 'Andés

As the sun fell below the horizon and the world below was shadowed in darkness, Miadrag and Waldo arrived at the City of Gold. It was the most amazing architecture Waldo had ever seen. The entire city was lit by a flood of light that made the city glow golden, even in the dark of the night. It was built in ancient Mayan tradition. The city's foundation was a large stone base consisting of an enormous stone square that stretched for half of a kilometre in both directions. In each of the four corners stood a huge frosted gold pyramid with shining gold polished caps. Between the pyramids were three sets of steps. Each set of steps led to a short landing, before another set of steps led to the next landing, followed by the third set of steps that led to the ground level of the city.

At the ground level, there were large stone walls with slotted rectangular square window slits, placed five metres apart. They encircled the square perimeter of the city behind. Beyond these walls, there were large structures that reached high into the sky. They all had sharp square symmetry and open square windows. Many of the tall structures had columns of over two hundred steps leading steeply up to large buildings, that sat on top of stepped triangular pyramid base structures. In the centre of the city was an enormous square building with large rectangular openings along its walls, each containing two large stone columns with square stone capping above the columns. Its extremities were intricately carved with hieroglyphics. The entire city was covered in gold gilding. It was truly a sight to behold.

Miadrag found a suitable clearing in a nearby wood and landed about half a kilometre away from the City of Gold. This was so that the Red Dragon, that was still guarding the city, would not detect them. It was dark in the wood, and Waldo wondered how he might see his way in the gloom. He also wondered how he might find Macey. It was such a large city, and he had no knowledge of where she was being held. Miadrag entering his thoughts said, "You have been given gifts Waldo, search for them." Waldo concentrated, but nothing happened. He relaxed his thoughts and focused clearly on his need to see. He kept focusing. He concentrated even harder. Ever so slowly he saw shadows and patches before him. A few seconds later, his eyes adjusted, and his vision came to him. He could see! It was as if the world had been cast in black and white, but he could see clearly enough.

"I can see Miadrag. I have moon-vision," laughed Waldo.

Miadrag smiled, "Good work Waldo."

Waldo, continuing the thought conversation, asked Miadrag about the fireball that the Salimandé had thrown at him. Miadrag asked, "Did it hit you Waldo?"

"Yes . . . in the shoulder, but I healed it with my palm. See how my shirt is in tatters from the blast," Waldo explained.

Miadrag responded, "You are learning fast Waldo. Why not try conjuring a fireball of your own?"

Waldo retorted, "A fireball! Don't you mean a moonball?"

"Mmm, try concentrating Waldo, and let's see what happens," coached Miadrag.

Waldo placed the palm of his hand upward in front of him and concentrated. He focused on what he thought a moonball might look like. To his amazement, the palm of his hand glowed white and a perfectly symmetrical ball the size of his hand in diameter appeared. It hovered in the free air whilst Waldo studied it. "Good work Waldo . . . now throw it at that rock under that tree over there," instructed Miadrag. Waldo threw the ball at the rock with pinpoint accuracy. After all, he was born in the country, and having a good aim was very handy in the country for lots of reasons.

The rock glowed shining white for a few minutes. Its light lit the forest area where they were standing before it petered out like a dying flame, and became a natutal looking rock again. "What do you think moonballs will do to people? Do you think they will hurt them?" asked Waldo.

"Well, experience tells me Waldo, that moonballs will not hurt good people, they will just fill them with love and happiness, but for evil people, moonballs will bring light into their black hearted souls. If there is even the smallest remnant of good inside of them, they may well be transformed and become good people again. If there is no good inside of them left, and they are truly evil, then moonballs like the amulet will search their souls for a place to release its energy. If it can't find one, then it will try to absorb the energy back into itself, and the moonballs will get exessively hot, and burn just as much as fireballs will," explained Miadrag.

"Mmm . . . well I guess all I need to be able to do now is find Macey, before it's too late. It is such a large city and there is so little time," worried Waldo. "Just follow your heart Waldo. Your love for her will take you to her," replied Miadrag. "You must go now Waldo. You have no time to lose. Keep your wits about you, and whatever you do, avoid the Red Dragon at all costs," instructed Miadrag. So Waldo left Miadrag in the wood. His black-and-white night vision enabled him to find his way through the tall trees and leaf-covered ground, avoiding the protruding tree roots and the bodies of the slain that littered the forest floor. The stench of their rotting corpses was unbearable.

Within a short time, Waldo was at the edge of the wood and was walking across the open field that led to the steps of the City of Gold. There were bodies everywhere, and the creatures of the night came out to feed on the fresh ones. There was a sinister looking creature that looked like a hairless monkey, only with sharp pointed triangular teeth and a long whip like tail. It's tail stood straight up into the air behind the beast, where it was always at the ready to strike. "It is a gargoyle," thought Waldo. The gargoyle spotted Waldo with its large protruding eyes. It hissed menacingly at him, as it protruded a long forked tongue through its razor-sharp teeth. It looked as if it was about to attack, but as Waldo's palm began to glow. The gargoyle sensed the danger, and it scurried away and disappeared into the forest. The moon was rising in the distance, and Waldo could feel his strength grow with every beam of moonlight that reached him.

As Waldo approached the city, the light reflecting from it lit the field. He no longer needed his night vision. Surprisingly, no one came out to challenge him, and the Red Dragon paid him little attention as it eyed him from above. Apparently, it had decided Waldo posed no threat, so he was allowed to walk right up to the city in plain view, just as all the other marauders did. Waldo walked up the three flights of steps and through one of the square openings in the wall that surrounded the city. Beyond this wall, was another wall, at the other side of a four-meter walkway. Further down to his right was another opening. It led to the gates of the city beyond.

Waldo walked to the gates that were over one hundred metres away. At the gates, the guards challenged him. They stopped him and frisked him for weapons. Since Waldo had none there was nothing to add to the great pile of weaponry that stood just inside the gate walls. "Put this on," he was told by one of the guards. He threw him a black hooded robe. Waldo caught it and put it on. He pulled the hood over his head and was allowed to walk freely through the gates. The last thing he heard from the guards was their sinister chuckles as he entered the city.

Inside the city, the walls were cold stone. The hieroglyphics etched into the walls were splattered with blood, some of it was fresh blood. Many of them had been vandalised as if someone had tried to chisel them out. Waldo could feel eyes watching him. Black hooded figures scurried this way and that. Some peered out menacingly from behind pillars, and others from nooks and crannies. The figures would pull back into the darkness as Waldo caught their gaze. There was the stench of dried blood that filled the air. It was rancid and overpowering. It made Waldo feel sick in the stomach. The air was so heavy and unpleasant it was hard to breathe.

Beyond the gates, there was a wide walkway that led up to a flight of steps. The steps then led upward to a large square building in the centre of the city. To the left and right, there were streets with tall stone housing on either side. The streets were straight and square. They had no curves at all, and they led like a maze, off in all directions. There were dead ends and connecting pathways all around—the dead ends were perfect places for ambush!

At first sight of the many paths to follow, Waldo didn't have any idea where he should go, but after concentrating for a few moments, he felt himself tuning into Macey's presence. He focused, and as he concentrated hard, he began to feel Macey's life force. He was able to tune into its location. She was alive! Macey was being held in the very centre of the city. Waldo walked straight down the wide walkway that led to the large flight of stairs, that then led upwards to cities centre.

The stairs lead up, to yet another platform. When Waldo was on top of this platform, he found himself about sixty meters in the air with panoramic views all around. Even in black and white, the mountains in the far distance looked magnificent.

Another ten meters further inside, there was another high stone wall, with doorways leading into it that serviced many places. Round columns bordered the entrance to all of them. Waldo walked through into the passageway beyond. The passageway was three metres wide. Just inside there was another passageway to the right and left that led in a large circle. There were doorways every fifty metres. The doorways lead into a large round open-air arena. There were steps leading downward and seats all around the amphitheatre for spectators to sit on. There was a grass field in the centre of the theatre at the bottom. It was in the middle of the arena. Judging by the blood spattered all around, this was a place where bloody battles to the death, and all manner of sinister events took place.

There was a stone wall about five metres high all around the inside of the arena, and at either end, there were barred gates that led to the catacombs and dungeons underneath it. Once on the field of the arena, there was no way in or out, except for the gates at each end. Waldo walked down the steps to the playing field wall. He jumped off the five-metre wall, to the grass floor of the arena below. As he did, he placed his arms out sideways. He wondered if he could fly. He floated down and landed gently at the bottom. He thought to himself, "Nice!"

He walked to the nearest barred gate. It was locked. He searched around the arena for something to pry it open. In one of the compartments underneath the wall was an arsenal of hand weapons. He took out a large bloodied axe. He took it back to the gate and swung it hard at the chained lock. As the steel axe hit the steel chain, sparks flew, and there was a resonating clang as the heavy axe struck the chain and bounced off. The noise from the metal striking metal at such force was extremely loud. It resonated the clang out into the dead of the night. It could have woken an entire army. Waldo dropped the axe and looked around, just in case someone had heard him. Someone did hear—the guards!

There were four guards who quickly unlocked the gate from the inside. Waldo realised in that moment that there was nowhere to run, so he would have to take his chances with the guards. He put his hands in the air and surrendered. The guards seized him. One of them scoffed at him in a gruff gravely voice, "Want to see the dungeons, eh boy?" They laughed as they led Waldo inside. The passages within the dark catacombs were lit with fiery torches. The guards led Waldo down many passageways until they came to a cell block, opened one of the cells there, threw Waldo into the cell and locked him inside.

Waldo wondered how he might escape. He looked around, but there was nothing he could use to free himself with. His position was looking somewhat grave. Somehow he managed to relax. He sat himself down to wait and see what would happen next. The room was made of bare stone. It had cold stone floors and walls, and nothing else. There was a guard at the end of the corridor on watch. The cell block that he was in contained four cells. Undoubtedly there would be hundreds of cell blocks like this one, he thought. It was pitch dark in his cell, but with his night vision, he could see that the other cells were empty. Waldo wished Miadrag was there, then he could ask him what to do next, but as hard as he tried he couldn't contact Miadrag with his thoughts.

Waldo sat in a corner and puzzled over what he might do next. After a short time had passed, the flickering light from a burning torch came down the corridor, and two guards appeared again. They opened the door and hustled Waldo out through a labyrinth of narrow passageways, until they emerged outside an ornately decorated temple. They took Waldo inside and threw him to the floor before leaving. Waldo struggled to find his feet. As he lifted his head up from the floor, Waldo found himself lying before the black and red painted face of the Salimandé. He was wearing a black hooded cloak, and his glowing red eyes were cold, and menacing. He glared at Waldo with an evil stare as he mocked him. "You shrivelling worm," he said. A shiver went down Waldo's spine.

"What were you doing in my arena, boy?" questioned the Salimandé. Waldo needed time to think. Stalling for time he thought for a moment and then responded, "I fell in, and I couldn't get out." Waldo stood up. The Salimandé roared at him, "How dare you stand up in my presence, you insolent dog!" His voice was booming loud. It was extremely frightening and every bit sinister! This guy really has a bad temper, thought Waldo. Waldo could see his hand glowing red, and a red hot fireball emerged. The Salimandé threw the fireball at Waldo, who quickly leapt to his right. It missed!

Waldo's scar began shining white as his thoughts prepared him for imminent battle. Waldo could feel the power of the moon fill him with strength. It was something he hadn't experienced before, and somehow he felt strong and invincible. His hand glowed. He conjured a moonball and threw it at the Salimandé, who simply wasn't expecting it. It hit him fair and square in the chest. The moonball passed straight through the Salimandé. His face squirmed, and he shrieked in pain as the sphere tried to fill the Salimandé's black cold heart with goodness. The Salimandé was strong. He put his hand over his wound and began to heal himself. Waldo summoned another moonball and threw it at the Salimandé. The Salimandé writhed with the force of the second direct hit, and his arm was rendered useless. The Salimandé squirmed and cowered in the corner. He put his good arm in the air over his face and begged Waldo for mercy. As Waldo summoned another moonball, the Salimandé begged him repeatedly, "Please, please, I'll do anything you wish, but please don't kill me," pleaded the Salimandé.

Waldo questioned, "Anything?"

"Yes, anything you want," said the cowering Salimandé lowering his arm.

"I want the girl you captured by the river today," said Waldo

"Yes—have her," said the Salimandé struggling to speak. He was in considerable pain.

"And I want the Great Book of Knowledge," said Waldo.

"Why you are an insolent pig," cried the Salimandé. He threw a fireball at Waldo. The Salimandé had been healing himself as he lay pretending to be weak. Waldo was unprepared, and the fireball hit him in the chest. The fireball was hot and it burnt Waldo's chest. He fell in a crumbling heap. He clasped his wound and quickly started healing himself. The Salimandé conjured fireball after fireball, and started throwing them at Waldo. Waldo's healing was fast as he drew power from the moon light that was streaming through the window. Waldo leapt behind a stone alter as fireballs blasted into the walls all around him.

The Salimandé was closing in on Waldo. He scrambled along the floor until he was at the opposite corner of the altar. Waldo was filled with emotions, confusing emotions of fear, anger and somehow love, all at the same time. Then as if by instinct, Waldo placed his outstretched arm out with the flat palm of his hand arched back as far as it would go, and he shouted, "Stop!"

The Salimandé was frozen still in a beam of light that radiated from Waldo's out stretched hand. It was a moon beam, and it froze the Salimandé in his tracks. The Salimandé was trapped motionless by the beam—he was helpless! Waldo conjured another moonball in his free hand, and carefully stood up to face the Salimandé. As he stood, he moved his palm and the moon beam shut off. The Salimandé now unfrozen, was quick to conjure more fireballs. So there they stood, face to face. They started throwing moonballs and fire balls in a viscous battle to the death. As the moonballs and fireballs hit each other, they exploded. Both Waldo and the Salimandé's arms were a flurry of activity as they launched ball after ball at each other. The balls thrown one for one hit each other and exploded one after the other, but as the battle wore on, they both began to tire. As they weakened, their rhythm no longer matched the other's. Some of the balls started to get through to their targets.

Waldo ducked and weaved to avoid being hit by the fireballs. As Waldo ducked and weaved he moved around the room. In one of these maneuvers, he found himself standing in the moon light that beamed through one of the stone windows in the room. His whole body lit up, and a sphere of bright light engulfed him. When the Salimandé's fireballs hit the sphere of light surrounding Waldo, they simply bounced off. Inside the safety of the sphere, Waldo grew stronger with every passing second. Whilst Waldo's strength was being returned at an accelerated rate, the Salimandé's strength was deminishing. Waldo sent a flurry of moonballs the Salimandé's way. The Salimandé did his best to deflect and intercept them with his return fireballs, but after a few minutes of this, the Salimandé started to weaken considerably. His strength had all but completely drained from him.

The sun was down. The Salimandé had no way of regaining his strength fast enough. Waldo, on the other hand, was being rapidly recharged by the moon. Even then, the Salimandé's strength was still considerable, and he fought on valiantly, but ever so slowly, Waldo wore the Salimandé down. Finally, the Salimandé was hit by three moonballs in a row. At that point, the Salimandé knew he was done for. He screamed for mercy. "Yes, anything you want. Take them! Take the girl and the Book, but you must spare me my life in exchange," the Salimandé squirmed. "Then take me to them," said Waldo. "One false move and I will finish you with this," threatened Waldo, bouncing a moon sphere in his palm. The Salimandé was in terrible pain. He was completely exhausted, and his body would need considerable amounts of direct sun light, in order to heal his wounds, and then to restore his strength. Waldo knew this time, that the Salimandé was truly beaten. He would not dare to try any more tricks, or he would risk certain death.

The Salimandé managed to drag himself up. He led the way, staggering from one wall to the other, into the adjoining room. Waldo stepped out of the moon light that was streaming through the window. The protective sphere of light surrounding him, disappeared. He followed the Salimandé with an ever watchful eye. He kept an eye out for even the slightest of false moves. In the next room, he found Macey. She was tied to an elaborately decorated stone slab. It was covered in sinister looking hieroglyphics. It was clearly a sacrificial table. When she saw Waldo enter the room, she didn't recognise him, as the black hooded cloak disguised him. The fact that he was holding a moonball, didn't put her at ease either. Waldo could see the fear in her eyes. He pulled off his robe and threw it on the floor. Macey's eyes lit up with excitement.

"Waldo . . . it's you!" she exclaimed. The Salimandé took a good look at Waldo and shouted, "You!" He lunged at Waldo and Waldo hit him with another moon ball. The Salimandé writhed with the pain and fell to the floor. The Salimandé was very weak now. One more moon sphere would surely finish him. Waldo hurriedly untied Macey, who instantly wrapped her arms around him, and kissed him passionately on the lips. Waldo kept his eyes on the Salimandé as he struggled to free himself from Macey's grasp. He exclaimed, "Not now Macey! We are still in very grave danger!"

He walked over to the Salimandé and demanded, "Now tell me . . . where is the Great Book of Knowledge?" He grabbed the Salimandé and dragged him to his feet. The Salimandé pointed towards another room, and then, now very, very weak, passed out and fell to the floor again. Waldo and Macey went into the next room, There in the middle of the room on a large stone pedestal, was a thick deeply embossed book. It was studded in precious gems and lined with silver gilding. On its cover were four large letters. The letters were embossed in shiny silver inside the familiar shape of the crescent moon. The letters read—"GBOK". Waldo took the book in his arms as he and

Macey fled quickly. When Waldo and Macey entered the altar room again, the Salimandé had gone. Waldo exclaimed, "He's gone to heal himself! We must hurry!"

Waldo and Macey ran outside. They were at the top level of the city. There were several hundred steps leading to the ground level and an open walkway below, that lead to the city gate. "Come Macey, this way . . . as fast as you can!" They both ran as swiftly as they could without falling, and they were soon at the walkway level and running between the buildings that lined either side. Another five minutes and they were approaching the city gates in full flight. No one had ever tried to leave the city before, so the guards were completely taken by surprise when the two of them came running straight out of the gates, down the three flights of steps and out across the open field towards the wood. In fact, the guards didn't seem to care at all. They simply shrugged at each other and returned to their post.

All the time they were running, Waldo clasped the Great Book of Knowledge tightly under his arm. Macey and Waldo made it to the middle of the field. The field was lit by the light from the glowing city of gold, so they could see where they were going quite well. They were running fast across the open field. Suddenly, a huge wall of flames came blasting down before them. It was the Red Dragon! It swooped low. They both leapt to the ground and rolled, to avoid the outstretched claws that were scooping down upon them. Waldo lost his grasp of the GBOK. He quickly spun around on his back, jumped to his feet, and started hurtling moonballs at the dragon. In a flurry of activity, Waldo littered the sky with shinning moon balls. It was a spectacular site to see.

Waldo kept hurtling moonballs in the general direction of the fast-moving dragon. As the Red Dragon turned to make its second pass at them, he slowed sufficiently on the turn for Waldo to get a slow enough target for him to aim accurately at. Waldo's moon balls hit the dragon's left wing, one after the other, completely immobilised it. With only one working wing, the Red Dragon was sent spiraling down. Its massive bulk spinning, as it hurtled towards the ground in a large open single winged swirl. The dragon crashed with a loud thud. It lifted its head momentarily in defiance. Two pitifully small flames fluttered meekly from its nostrils, before it became unconscious, and its head fell to the ground motionless.

Waldo picked up the GBOK. He and Macey ran for their lives, for whilst the dragon was wounded and unconscious, they expected it wouldn't be staying that way for too long. They ran for another five minutes. They made it back to the relative safety of the dark wood. The moon was high in the sky now, so it bathed the woods in enough light for Macey to partly see by, but still the going was slow. Waldo led Macey by the hand. It was important that they kept moving. Their hearts were pounding with fear, and Macey's body ached with exhaustion. They pressed on. It wasn't too long before they found their way back to Miadrag. Miadrag was overjoyed when he saw Macey. When he saw the great book, he could barely contain his exuberance. He kept repeating, "Well done Waldo! Well done!"

"We must leave quickly Miadrag," Waldo urged. He helped Macey climb onto the dragon's back. Waldo also climbed on Miadrag's back, clasping tightly to the GBOK at the same time. Macey wrapped her arms around Waldo's waist and held on tight. She cuddled him and thanked him for saving her. Miadrag rose into the moonlit air, and flew off at great speed. Miadrag congratulated Waldo again, "Well you actually did it. You have the Great Book of Knowledge Waldo." Miadrag continuing as he questioned, "How did you ever manage to get the Book and Macey out of the city Waldo?" Waldo filled Miadrag in with all the details. Miadrag mused at Waldo's cleverness. Getting the Salimandé to give Waldo, Macey and the book, allowed Waldo to keep his integrity. Being pure of thought, the city had no choice, but to grant Waldo and Macey safe passage through its evilness. They were the first ones ever, to escape its satanic grasp.

Waldo turned to Macey. "Macey are you alright? Did they hurt you?" he asked.

Macey replied, "I'm ok Waldo. The Salimandé took me to that room and tied me to the stone table. I have been lying there ever since. From time to time, the priests would come in and make preparations around me. The priests rattled feathery things in my face, and chanted in a strange language, but they didn't touch me other than that. Waldo was relieved.

Waldo asked, "Are you taking us back to Macey's village Miadrag?"

"Yes Waldo," replied Miadrag, "We must warn the village that the Salimandé will surely seek revenge. He will destroy the village as well as every living thing in it," explained Miadrag.

It was a few hours later when they arrived back at the village. The village folk couldn't believe their eyes when they saw Macey safe and sound again. They crowded around Macey, and there was much cuddling and cheering. "Well done Waldo," said Macey's father, giving him a huge manly bear hug. Then, as the questions came thick and fast for Waldo to explain how he rescued Macey, the dragon interrupted, "Sorry to break things up, but the Salimandé will return as soon as he can, which could be shortly after the sun rises, so you all need to pack up and leave as quickly as you can."

The villagers agreed, and within the hour, they had gathered all of their worldly goods, and were starting to move out. The villagers also knew, that neither the village nor Macey would be safe if she stayed with the village, as the Salimandé would search for her in every village until he found her. Once he found her, he would destroy both her, and everyone and everything around her. Without Macey, the village could blend in. They would simply be another village, just like all the other villages around them. Without Macey, the Salimandé would not be able to link them to her, and he would have no interest in them whatsoever. They would be safe. So it needed to be, that when the villagers were ready to go, they said their good-byes to Macey, Waldo and Miadrag, and the two parties went their separate ways, leaving in totally different directions.

Waldo packed the Great Book of Knowledge in his backpack and put it on his back. He had to get Macey to sit on the dragon's back in front of him, as the backpack would otherwise get in her way as she tried to hold onto Waldo. He quite liked it this way though, and he held Macey tightly in his arms as she held onto the dragon's neck. She was warm, and her hair was soft. She smelt so good. Waldo held her and cuddled her as his feelings for her overwhelmed him. He felt such joy to have her back with him once more . . . he had nearly lost her, and that was something he never wanted to do, ever again. The dragon flew quickly into the night air, and they were soon out of sight of the villagers. Waldo asked, "Where shall we go now Miadrag?" Miadrag replied exuberantly, "To the Silver City Waldo! Mine, and now yours and Macey's new home. It is also where we need to return the Great Book of Knowledge, restore power to the city, and peace and harmony to the land."

They flew for a few more hours. As the dawn broke and the sun shone in Waldo's eyes, Waldo felt very tired. The events of the past night had finally caught up with him, as his relaxed state relinquished him to the extreme tiredness he suddenly felt. Waldo asked, "Can we rest soon?" It was almost twenty-four hours since his last sleep. Miadrag, although uncomfortable, knew they were sufficiently far enough away from the City of Gold, to be safe now. He had deliberately picked a round-about route to the Silver City, so that even using orbs, the dragon and the Salimandé would only ever find them through chance. Miadrag found a suitable forest clearing with enough cover for them to seek refuge in. He landed, and they all took shelter under the cover of the tall trees there.

Waldo lay out the bed on the ground under a tree nearby. Waldo slept holding Macey in his arms. The dragon kept watch.

Waldo and Macey slept soundly until the early afternoon. When they awoke, they were hungry, so they ate some of the food that they had been given to them by the villagers. After they had finished eating, Waldo packed up their camp bed, and packed the backpack. When it came to packing the Great Book of Knowledge, Waldo and Macey couldn't contain their curiosity any longer. They ran over to the dragon who was lying on his stomach on the ground. As they sat on the ground, their backs up against the dragon's front shoulder, they rested the book between them, and together with great expectations, they very carefully opened it.

The dragon smiled when they found nothing, but two blank glassy pages inside the GBOK's covers. Waldo exclaimed, "It's empty Miadrag!" Waldo's and Macey's eyes and mouths had pooped wide open in disbelief. "As it should be Waldo," explained the dragon. "The GBOK is merely a communication medium. Networks of Books are linked to each other, and together they are able to gather and store all history and information known to the universes, past and present. It needs to be returned to the Pedestal of Light before it can work again. Once reconnected through the Pedestal of Light networks, only then can it channel and link to the information and memories that are floating out there as they travel through time and space. "This is why we must go to the Silver City," explained Miadrag, "We must return the Great Book to the Pedestal of light. Once this is done the Silver City, and the GBOK will be restored to its former glory."

Waldo and Macey finished packing and jumped on Miadrag's back. The dragon flapped his giant wings, and the trio were off on their journey once more. The sun was high in the sky as the dragon flew with great speed. After another six hours of travelling, the sun set, and a few more hours after that the moon rose. Flying at night in the moonlight was one of the dragon's most favourite things to do. The air was fresh, and they could travel undetected. The Salimandé would have no way of finding them as they flew high above the clouds across the moon light skies.

In a few more days they would be safe in the Silver City. The Silver City is a moon city. As one might expect, the city derives its power from the moon. Unlike the Sun City, it is full of good and kind people, and Miadrag knew that Waldo and Macey would feel very much at home there. Until now, the trio barely had any time to catch their breath. Fresh with a good sleep, and the time to ponder the things that happened, Macey began to think things through, and she began to wonder. How was Waldo able to fight the Salimandé and win? How could he do all those things she saw him do? She recalled that the last time she saw him, he was injured by the river. Now, whilst his shirt was in tatters, his shoulder was completely healed. There were no signs of any injuries whatsoever. In fact, there wasn't even a scar left from the arrow that pearced his shoulder either.

Macey asked Waldo how these things came to pass, and as they flew, Waldo and the dragon explained to Macey how Waldo had become the Maligrandé, and that he had been given gifts, some of which he was yet to discover. Somehow Macey wasn't too surprised, for she had seen how quickly Waldo had healed from the arrow. She had also thought when she first saw it, that the scar on Waldo's chest, was something very special. In any case, it was clear she was in good hands now. The stories Miadrag and Waldo told her, made her feel-good inside. Macey now felt even safer than before. It was great to be in Waldo's and Miadrag's care.

For the next few days, the trio travelled at night and slept during the daytime. During the day, after resting, Macey and Waldo would play, and the dragon loved to watch them laugh and giggle. On occasion, they would bring their lips together in tender moments. The two of them loved to swim in the rivers that they camped by. When they were hungry, they would eat and drink sparingly from their supplies, which would be enough to get them to the Silver City, if they used them wisely. At the end of each day, as the night fell across the land, they would pack their belongings, and be on their way again.

It was around 1:00am in the early morning of the third night of their travels. As they flew high in the night sky, they could see the very first, ever so faint sparkles, from lights in distant houses. As they drew closer, the lights formed an immense circle about twenty kilometres across. The city lights rose into the sky in three distinct tiers. With each level to the city's lights, there was a slight tapering in towards the highest level. At the very top of the city, there was a large black area where there were no lights to be seen at all. When Macey saw the distant lights, she exclaimed with excitement, "Waldo, Miadrag . . . look, the Silver City!" They all admired it from their vantage point high in the sky, and as they flew, their hearts rose with anticipation. They pondered on how magnificent it must be, and how wonderful it must be living there. After a few more hours of flying, the sun started to rise. Miadrag was taking no chances with the Salimandé and the Red Dragon which could be lying in wait for them, so the trio found a place to camp and rest for the day. Waldo and Macey were so excited. They could hardly get to sleep, but after a while, they nodded off and slept. The city was still half a days flying time away, so this would be the last stopover on their journey there.

The Reluctant King

espite their excitement, Waldo and Macey slept for a solid eight hours. As soon as they woke, they packed and urged Miadrag to continue their journey. It was still broad daylight, but since they were now so close, even Miadrag was eager to get to the Silver City. Macey and Waldo climbed aboard Miadrag's back, and they flew off. The city from the distance was the size of a small hill on the horizon. It had a shining silver light radiating from its top. Even from a far, the city was enchanting in its dazzling beauty.

As the afternoon progressed, the sun sunk lower in the sky. The city changed colour with the setting sun. It changed from silver, as it reflected all the vivid colours of the sunset. As they drew closer, the outline of the Silver City came into plain view. In the daylight, the large rings that formed the three tiers, that created the three levels of the city, could now be clearly seen. The perimeter of the city was encircled with a huge, smooth silver lined wall. There were eight symmetrical gateways, that led through to eight symmetrically spaced streets. These led in straight lines through to the top level of the city. Each tier was joined by stairways with side ramps. They led to the next level of the city. Waldo and Macey were amazed to see that the top of the city wasn't actually flat at all, instead, the city was capped with the most elaborate silver palace that you will ever see. It was simply stunning to look at. As it reflected the colours of the sunset, it became even more beautiful.

At each end of the palace, and in the middle, as well as to either side of the great and extravagant facade which formed the palace's grand entrance, there were large rounded turrets that protruded skyward in perfect symmetry. At each end, the turrets were capped with tastefully decorated spires. The main building was four stories high, and it was several hundred meters in length. It had symmetrically spaced windows with six crystal panes per window, lining each level. In the middle of the palace above the area between the turrets, either side of the grand entrance, a cacophony of towers rose skyward above the fourth story roof line. The spires were in duplicate to match and balance both sides. Beyond these towers were three more magnificent spires. At its very core was a duel staircase that was like none other. It was a shiny polished silver double helix staircase that surrounded a central circular core. It led from the bottom level of the palace to its apex. From directly above, the entire palace was perfectly symmetrical. It was covered in polished silver that shone like a mirror in the sunlight. Its bright reflection dazzled onlookers with its striking brilliance.

Miadrag flew right over the city. People ran out of their houses, and they made a great commotion with cheers and shouts. Clearly, they were pleased to see the dragon return. Indeed, Miadrag was well pleased with his reception. It was plain to see, that the people truly loved him. Miadrag headed straight for the Silver Palace. As the sun set, he landed in a courtyard that looked like it had been built specifically for him. It was like a dragon landing pad. Waldo and Macey jumped down from Miadrag's back.

The palace's main entrance was huge. It was shaped in a high arch. It and the corridors beyond were so large that the dragon could easily walk inside the palace. "Come along Waldo, Come along Macey, quickly follow me, we don't have a moment to loose," urged Miadrag. He led them through the dark corridors. Macey held tightly onto Waldo's hand. She could hardly see anything at all in the pitch darkness of the unlit castle corridors. Miadrag led them to a great domed room that was at the very centre of the palace. The room was directly below the city's central spire that marked the very middle of the entire city. There in the middle of the domed room, there was a beautifully and elaborately carved stone pedestal. "Quickly Waldo, place the Great Book on the Pedestal," instructed Miadrag, "Once it is in place, the city will be safe from the Salimandé and the Red Dragon, and all other threats, for that matter," urged Miadrag.

Waldo took off his backpack and took out the Great Book. Carefully, he carried it over to the Pedestal of Light. It was standing in the middle of a magnificent mosaic of polished marble floor. Waldo took great care as he placed the Great Book on the Pedestal's tilted top. The top was specifically made to take the book. It was angled at sixty degrees. The pedestal's surface contained a shallow rectangular recess that the Great Book's cover fitted perfectly into. Waldo placed the book into the recess and stepped back, but nothing happened.

"Open the book Waldo," instructed Miadrag. Waldo opened the front cover of the book, and in the same instant, the GBOK glowed. A great flood of light streamed out of the books optical glass pages, sending a beam of bright white-light upward that shot straight up into the ceiling above. The light then passed through a hole at the very apex of the dome. Once the light hit the apex, it was channeled through a conduit that led straight up to the top of the central spire. From there, the spire's cap dispersed the light to form a perfect dome. The dome covered the perimeter with a film of shining white light all around the city from the apex, to the ground in its entirety. The dragon explained to Macey and Waldo, that the dome of light formed an impenetrable force field that protected the city from attackers. Additionally, if anything tries to move through the light field, it is scanned by the GBOK. Anything that shouldn't have access is denied entry, and unable to pass through the field into the city. In this way, if anything evil tried to gain entry to the city, it will be instantly prevented from entering. With the GBOK and Pedestal of Light doing their job, the city was indeed, perfectly safe and secure once more.

The palace was also flooded with light once more. Every room lit up to reveal the magnificence and the great craftsmanship that had pain stakingly built it. It was overpowering. Waldo and Macey were stunned. The murals that adorned the domed ceiling were astonishing, and the gold and silver gilded trims that formed the many ornate arches and lace work across the ceilings, was superbly crafted. The cold air in the palace began to warm as the city's heating began working again. Outside of the palace, there was a huge commotion that could be heard from inside the palace, as the people celebrated with jubilation and merriment, the return of the GBOK and the restoration of power to the great city.

The streets, were now lit with a flood of light, and the people had already begun to dance and cheer, as they celebrated. "Come you two, we must get you ready to meet the people," said Miadrag. He led them to another part of the palace where there were clothes of such finery, that they could hardly believe their eyes. "Here Waldo, this is the traditional dress of the Maligrandé, and this Macey is for you," instructed Miadrag. The two of them changed their clothes. Waldo emerged wearing a full-length white hooded robe, with long deep angled shining silver cuffs. It was embossed with gold and silver lacings, and it had the round emblem of the Moon Dragon wrapped around the crescent moon in silver, just below the left shoulder. The robe had a silver lining, and Waldo looked absolutely magnificent in it. When Macey emerged, Waldo was quite taken aback. She was wearing a shining silver full-length crushed panne gown, with a gold lame front panel, sheer sleeve drapes, silver wrist to elbow sleeves, sequin trim, and a magnificent solid silver tiara, studded with sets of perfect blue diamonds. Macey looked absolutely stunning. Miadrag exclaimed with extreme delight, "Perfect!"

Waldo took Macey by the arm, and the two of them followed Miadrag to the palace's grand entrance where a great crowd had gathered to greet them. When they saw Macey, Waldo and the dragon emerge, they cheered and cheered. Macey and Waldo made the perfect couple, and the crowd loved them at once. As Waldo and Macey walked through the cheering crowd, his scar shone brightly through his robe. When the people saw the light shining from his chest, they knew straight away that Waldo was truly the Maligrandé. Their world was complete. This was indeed a time, for much celebration!

Indeed, it was a time for great rejoicing. The people lined the streets as Waldo and Macey riding on Miadrag's back, paraded firstly down one street, and then the next. When the trio had finished parading, they joined in the festivities, and the abundant food. As they ate, they chatted with the people, and after they finished eating and chatting, they danced to the music playing as well. They laughed and danced all through the night, until finally, the dawn sun rose. The people tired and returned to their homes. It was a huge night that would be well remembered by all.

The dragon took Macey and Waldo back to the palace. On the way there, Miadrag told Waldo and Macey how the palace was built many centuries ago in preparation of the coming of the Maligrandé. As the true Maligrandé, the palace was now their home, and they could live there, for as long as they wished. Waldo and Macey couldn't believe their ears. Waldo queried Miadrag, "You mean this is our home now?" "Yes," replied Miadrag, "But with the palace comes this kingdom. You Waldo are by your re-birth as the Maligrandé, the rightful ruler of this land. Should you accept this kingdom, you will also be accepting the responsibility for its people, and you must rule the land as the Maligrandé and as its righteous king." The dragon then led Macey and Waldo to one of the royal bed chambers. He left them there. He then walked to his own bed chamber, which was an astonishingly adorned lair, lined with precious gems, and all the things that dragons loved and cherished. Miadrag settled down and slept. It was the first time he slept soundly, in five million years.

Macey looked around the magnificent bed chamber as they lay on the bed with its rich robes, and fine linen. She said to Waldo, "Pinch me Waldo," as she soaked in the exquisite finery in the room. "Can you believe this is true Waldo? Are we dreaming? Can this really be true?" Waldo smiled at her. She looked simply gorgeous, as her eyes sparkled in her excitement. He pulled her close to him and kissed her, and she kissed him back. They snuggled into bed and were soon fast asleep. The night's festivities were fabulous, but coupled with their long ordeal, very exhausting. It wasn't until the morning of the following day, did they wake.

It was early morning. Waldo and Macey found fresh clothes had been laid out for them, so they dressed and began exploring the palace's many rooms and chambers. The palace was filled with exotic arches and awnings. There were exquisite paintings, murals and gold and silver gilding adorning the ceilings and walls. There were magnificent mosaic tiled floors, and marble pillars and statues everywhere. Waldo and Macey ran from room to room giggling and sighing, as they explored from one end to the other of each level, of this grand palace. At one point, they stumbled across Miadrag's lair. Miadrag was fast asleep. He was snoring with hot bursts of air, with the odd lashings of flames that flickered as they came out of his nostrils. Waldo and Macey chuckled, tiptoed out, and quickly ran off to explore some more.

On another occasion, they came across the kitchen where there were many kitchen hands fussing away cooking and preparing a great feast for someone, obviously someone very important. Macey asked the chef, "Who is coming to lunch?"

The chef replied, "Why, you are your hignesses." He proclaimed with delight, "A meal fit for a King and Queen!" Waldo checked his watch. It was 11:30am.

"What time is lunch?" he asked.

"Twelve-thirty sharp, in the Great Dining Hall," replied the chef. Waldo and Macey ran off. The chef gave a big smile at the two of them running off enjoying themselves. He returned to his work. He and his team would be working frantically to have everything ready on time.

At twelve-thirty, Macey and Waldo turned up at the Great Dining Hall. They walked in quite matter of fact. There was a great gathering there, so they tried to walk straight and tall and act as pompous as they could, but they merely burst out laughing. They totally relaxed, which suited them much better in any case. Waldo noticing that all eyes were suddenly on the two of them, as an old tallish thin man, with long silver-grey flowing hair, and a deeply wrinkled face came over to them. He was dressed in royal robes, and he introduced himself as the Caretaker. He escorted them to the two grand chairs that sat side by side in the middle of a great head table. The head table stretched horizontally across the grandest end of the room. As the two took their places, the gathering broke its silence, and returned to their conversations. Their chatter warmed the room.

The great hall was filled with round tables as far as the eye could see. There were at least five hundred people already seated in the room. As the old man stood up and walked over to the magnificent marble podium to the side of the head table, the room fell silent. The Caretaker made a great speech. He welcomed Waldo and Macey to the palace. He then blessed them, and he thanked God for bringing the Maligrandé, Macey, the GBOK and Miadrag back to them, and restoring the city to its former glory. He proclaimed that with Miadrag, Waldo and Macey, and the return of the Great Book of Knowledge, that the entire kingdom would now prosper, and be at peace once more.

After the Caretaker resumed to his seat, the great feast began. It continued for several more hours. The Caretaker explained to Waldo and Macey, that he was in a long line of caretakers whose responsibility it was, to maintain the palace and care-take the kingdom, until the Maligrandé returned. He added that it was his great honour to be the one who would finally hand over the rule to the rightful king. Macey was delighted and very proud. Waldo had some thinking to do. The idea of being king had some merit Waldo thought, but he needed more time to give it some more serious consideration. After all, he didn't quite know what might be required of him.

When the lunch feast was over, the Caretaker told Waldo that he would await them in the Great Throne Room, and that he and Macey should join him when they were ready. Waldo agreed to meet the Caretaker there, not even knowing where the Throne Room was. Waldo and Macey left as everyone else started leaving. The two lovers ran off excitedly to explore the yet undiscovered secrets of the palace.

The palace was full of people, all of whom seemed to be dedicated to one task or another. Whenever the two came across someone new, they would ask politely their names, and what they did. The responses were always very polite in return, and given with a smile. It was a bit disconcerting for Waldo at first, as people referred to them as your majesties, but after a while, he got used to it. Waldo accepted that this was what the people wanted to call them. He even began to enjoy their sincere attentions.

It wasn't until Waldo and Macey stumbled across the Great Throne Room on the fourth floor, that the reality of being rulers over the land, became much clearer to the young couple. As they entered the throne room, they were overwhelmed by the two glistening silver thrones that sat at the head of the large magnificently decorated hall, before them. The hall had gold and silver trappings everywhere. Above the thrones, the ceiling formed a great painted dome. The paintings were of the finest quality, and may well have been painted by Michelangelo himself. As they entered the room, they were both given the white, silver and gold, royal robes, complete with the Maligrandé's silver emblem embossed on them, for them to wear.

Waldo and Macey placed their arms into their respective garments, as assistants raced to help place the robes on them. The Caretaker came over and said, "Very good." He led them over to the thrones and motioned for them to be seated. Once seated the room was filled with the most beautiful voices singing. It sounded so perfect, that it could well have been heaven's angels themselves that were singing. Waldo looked up. On either side of the long throne room, in the arched balconies above, the singers in the choir were standing as they sang. They were dressed in white with tall silver headdresses, that protruded out in a symmetry of falling silver reeds. Sparkling crystals from their sequined clothing glinted in the light as they sang, and rainbows of colour flashed around the room, with their slightest of movements.

The singing continued as the great doors to the throne room were opened, and the procession of people came forward. The people came forward in single file, and one by one, they knelt before the two seated before them. They took Waldo's right hand and Macey's left hand. They placed them both on their foreheads as they knelt before them with their heads bowed and their eyes closed. To Waldo's amazement as they did so, his hand would glow. He felt the great warmth of their love overcome him. Waldo's people truly did love him, and through this simple ritual, Waldo also discovered his great love for his people So it was for the next few days that the entire city, every man, woman and child, old and young, came before Waldo and Macey to receive, and to give their blessings. They continued this great ritual in session after session, until all the subjects within the kingdom had been to meet their rightful King, and his chosen one.

This was how it all began, and the kingdom awoke to its new beginnings with a true and rightful king to love it, and guide it, to heal its wounds, and to protect it. With every day that passed Waldo watched the city's glow get brighter and brighter, as its people grew stronger. Their lives became happy and complete again. As the days passed by the dragon slept on, never waking, not even for an instant, yet as he slept, Miadrag also began to shine brighter and brighter until he was shining so brightly, that he gave off a silver aura that surrounded him in a great silvery haze. Waldo and Macey would check on the dragon everyday. Waldo missed being able to talk to Miadrag as he thought more and more about being king, and what it meant to his people.

One day, Waldo and Macey were in the centre tower looking at the glorious view of the kingdom. There were vast green rolling hills and distant mountains, that stretched out beyond the silver dome as far as the eye could see. Indeed, it was a peaceful and beautiful land to behold. They could see villagers working in the pastures below. The Caretaker came to them and said, "I have been sent to ask you if you have made a decision on taking up your rightful role in the kingdom Waldo? It has been several weeks now, and the people are anxious to crown their new king. It is time Waldo to decide if you are going to accept this great honour."

Waldo replied, "Truly this is a great honour Caretaker, but I haven't been able to accept . . . I don't know what it is, but something is holding me back."

The Caretaker responded, "I am indeed truly sorry to hear that Waldo, but you must know that a kingdom without a king cannot grow, it simply withers, and eventually it will die. This is what happened to us before . . . now the people have been filled with such hope, but nothing has come of it. The people are growing restless. This is your kingdom Waldo, and you must make your choice as to what your part in it will be. We need you Waldo, and we want you Waldo. I have been sent by the people to ask you, Waldo, will you be our king?"

Waldo thought for a long moment as he stared into the distance. Truly, the time to decide was finally upon him. He could feel the pressure and the great expectations of the entire kingdom pressing on him. It weighed heavily upon his conscience. Waldo thought for a moment, "I must consult with The Great Book," he finally replied.

"Very well," said the Caretaker. "Let it be so." The Caretaker bowed slightly before Waldo. "Come," he said, "Let us go to the Pedestal of Light." So the trio went to the great domed room where the Great Book of Knowledge lay on the Pedestal of Light.

"What do I do Caretaker?" asked Waldo.

"Place your hands on the open pages of the Book Waldo and the Book will speak with you." Waldo walked over to the Great Book and placed his left hand on the page to the left, and his right hand on the page to the right. The book glowed. He could hear the soft soothing voice of a woman speaking to him inside of his head.

The voice spoke to him, just like his thought conversations with the dragon. "Ah Waldo, how I have waited such a long time to talk with you. The centuries have passed so slowly, but finally, my waiting is over, and you are here at last."

"Amazing," thought Waldo.

The Book spoke, "Is there something, in particular, I may be able to help you with, Waldo?"

"Yes," replied Waldo. "I do not know what I should do. I feel a great weight of responsibility on my shoulders, and I am afraid I cannot decide on what is the best thing for me to do. I really don't want to disappoint anyone."

The Book answered, "How could the Maligrandé disappoint anyone, Waldo? You have become a great and powerful being,

Waldo. Your heart is true, and you love, and are loved by your people. What more could a king want Waldo?"

Waldo asked, "Then why am I feeling so unsure of myself? Something just doesn't feel right"

"A very good question Waldo. Indeed why are you unsure? You must follow your heart Waldo."

"I don't think I am ready to be king," Waldo blurted out.

"Then you aren't ready to be King Waldo. Tell them that," the Book said.

"Clearly you have unfinished business that troubles you. You must deal with that, for until you do, you will never be able to move forward. Unfinished business will always hold you back."

Waldo enquired, "What must I do before I am free, with a clear conscience, to decide?"

"You must resolve your issues with your past Waldo. Only then you will be able to decide on your future Waldo," advised the Book.

Waldo questioned, "Do you mean I must go home to Earth?"

"Earth?" The book questioned, "Ah . . . there you go Waldo. Home is where your heart is. Where does your heart truly lie Waldo? Where do you want to be Waldo? Is it here on Annulus, or is it were you grew up on Earth?"

"I really don't know," replied Waldo. "I love them both."

"Then you must find out," insisted the Book.

"I just don't know what has happened with my family on Earth. Maybe they are still out there looking for me, and what will become of me, and can ever I go back?" Waldo began prattling.

"Here Waldo, take this." A round shining crystal band appeared on Waldo's wrist. "It is a transgression band. With it, I can transport you anywhere you want to go. You can also talk to me whenever you activate it, no matter where you are. I can now transport you back to your birthplace if you wish, but know this Waldo, when the band is removed the transmission link is broken. Once the link is lost, I cannot communicate, or transport you. Well not until the link is re-established once more. You can do that, by simply putting it on and wearing it again. The problem is, if you become separated from the band, you will be trapped, at least until you can get it back," warned the book.

The Book continued, "To activate the band, all you have to do is clasp it, and we will be able to talk as we are now." Waldo felt relief. He was getting excited about being able to return to Earth again.

Waldo sought reassurance, "You mean I really can go back?"

"Yes Waldo. All you have to do is clasp the band, and tell me where you want to go. I will then transport you there. Remember Waldo, whenever you wish to speak with me, all you need to do from this day forward, is to activate the band in the same way, by clasping it," instructed the Book.

The voice faded as the conversation ceased. Waldo took his hands off of the pages of the Great Book. He instinctively clasped his left wrist with his right to get a feel for the band. The band glowed. "Yes Waldo, what is it?" the Book's voice spoke in a soft slow soothing tone.

"Oops, I accidentally clasped the band . . . eh sorry," he conversed in his thoughts.

"Anytime . . . just clasp if you need me," said the voice as it faded away. The band stopped glowing.

"Waldo, what happened?" ask Macey excitedly.

"The book spoke with me in my mind, and it gave me this band. I can talk with it anytime I want to now, and it can take me anywhere I want to go," Waldo replied.

The Caretaker interrupted, "So what say you Waldo—will you be King?"

"Waldo looked into Macey's eyes as he said, "I cannot."

Macey exclaimed, "What are you saying Waldo!"

"I am not ready. I must go back to my place of birth. I must choose my destiny from there," replied Waldo.

Macey pleaded with Waldo anxiously, "You can't Waldo. I can't bear to be without you. Take me with you . . . please Waldo take me with you."

A tear rolled down Waldo's cheek as he said, "I can't. This is something I know I must do alone, but if ever there was a reason in the entire universe for me to return quickly, it is for you Macey." He drew her to him, and he cuddled her.

"So be it," said the Caretaker. "You must go now, Waldo. Go and deal with your past. Only then will you be able to decide your future path. We shall await your return Waldo, go with god's speed my liege."

Macey in her extreme distress, begged Waldo again, "Please Waldo, please, please don't leave me." Macey was utterly distraught. How could he leave her like this? Her tears streamed down her cheeks as she couldn't believe this was happening. "Waldo must go alone Macey," soothed the Caretaker.

Waldo clasped the band as he said to Macey, "I love you Macey." He told the Book, that he was ready. He shimmered, and disappeared. The Book transported him back to Earth. Macey's heart sank. She ran off screaming, "No! No! No!" The Caretaker's heart sank to, but he knew this was the way it had to be.

In Waldo's absence, the city mourned. The people wept for the return of their king, and they prayed for his safe return every day that passed. The dragon never woke, even though Macey tried and tried to get him to wake, he wouldn't wake, no matter what she did. The city's glow dulled, and the dragon's aura faded with every new day. On the fourth day, the dragon's aura disappeared completely, and the city's glow became nothing but a faint dull hue. Macey was in the tower pining for her true love, and hoping Waldo would suddenly return, but in the hours and days and weeks that passed, Waldo never returned.

Macey's tears rolled down her cheeks as she sobbed for her lost love. In her distress and her sadness, she sought solitude. She found that the loneliness of the tower provided her with a place that she could go, and pour out her deep sadness without anyone knowing. Macey tried to keep up appearances, but it was so lonely without Waldo. Macey questioned in her thoughts, "Why hasn't he returned?" Something terrible must have happened, she thought to herself. The thought of Waldo never being able return, made her deeply distressed, and she cried out even more loudly in her despair.

After a while, Macey could cry no more. She composed herself ready to return to face the people in the palace once again. She so hoped that they wouldn't be able to tell how sad she really was. She practiced her pretend smiles. Macey took a moment to survey the horizon, and she thought positive thoughts to help compose herself. As she was staring into the distance, she noticed that a huge black cloud of dust was billowing up into the distant sky towards the horizon, still a long way off. She watched as ever so slowly the dust cloud moved closer, and she wondered what it could be. It was then she noticed a black dot flying through the air in front of the dust cloud. The terrifying reality of what was heading towards the city became suddenly clear to Macey. She forgot her sadness as she was overcome with fear, for she knew exactly what it was.

It was the Red Dragon she could see flying through the sky and with it would be the Salimandé. The dust cloud was from the advancing army as it charged across the land to lay siege on the Silver City. Macey's heart sank as she ran to raise the alarm—the city was under siege! The city quickly prepared for the assault that was heading its way. Messengers were sent out to the far reaches of the kingdom, to warn the people living there of the looming attack. All the people that lived outside of the city's protective dome, raced to take refuge inside it. As soon as everyone was inside, the city's gates were sealed shut. The only thing left to do now, was sit and wait.

The Demise of Waldo and the Sliver City

aldo having been transported back to Earth, shimmered and reappeared by the narrow dam to the right of Grannies Lane. It was the exact spot he had been transported from in the beginning. His bike was lying on the ground, just as he had left it. Waldo mounted his bike. He could hardly believe it . . . he was home! He was so excited that he took off at high speed and raced off across the paddock and back towards the gravel road of Grannies Lane.

Waldo hoped no one had missed him yet. He was so excited about being home. Waldo's head was so filled with thoughts of what was going to happen when he was finally re-united with his family again, that he didn't even notice the dark shadow racing across the ground behind him. It raced up behind him and was quickly overtaking him. By the time Waldo realised something was wrong, it's dark shadow had engulfed him—it was way too late!

Waldo glanced back towards the rush of air he could hear in the sky coming up fast behind him. There to his horror, just five metres away now, was the Red Dragon swooping down

upon him at high speed. The last thing Waldo saw, was the red
hot ball of fire and plumes of black smoke, that came pouring
out of the dragon's mouth towards him. The fire ball engulfed
him entirely. The heat was so intense, that Waldo was instantly
incinerated. Waldo incurred serious burns to all parts of his
body. He fell to the ground in a smoking pile of burnt flesh
and charred bone. The Red Dragon flew on for a short distance
to satisfy himself that the job was done. The dragon glanced
back at Waldo's smouldering remains before shimmering and
was gone.

Waldo was in extreme agony. His body was reeling in pain
as it struggled to hang onto its last threads of life. He could
feel the unrelenting sting of his burns. His head throbbed as
his brain tried to cope. It sent his body into shock. He shivered
all over. His charred body smelt of burnt flesh. His skin was
mottled black and pink as blisters formed. Waldo tried to reach
out and heal himself, but he was too weak. He passed out.

When Waldo didn't come home for lunch, his family
began to worry. Waldo's Dad began searching for him. He first
searched the paddocks across the road, and then he searched
the paddocks in Grannies Lane. It wasn't long before he found
Waldo's charred body. Waldo's dad carried him to the car and
raced him to the hospital, were he was placed in the Critical
Burns Unit. The doctors didn't think there was much hope for
Waldo, for he had fourth-degree burns over eighty percent of
his body. No-one ever recovered from such serious injuries.

Waldo lay in a coma for four days. With every passing hour,
Waldo's body grew weaker as it struggled to cope with the
massive burns it had received. In his coma, his thoughts flashed
back to his time with Macey. He relived the great love that had
grown between them. He couldn't help but feel how foolish he
had been. He couldn't bare the thought of never seeing Macey
again. He fought with all his might. He was determined that he
would survive. He was very brave, but he was so very weak.
He was using all of his strength simply to hang on.

Waldo managed to hang on for many days more than expected. The hospital was surprised he had survived such serious injuries for so long, but they held little hope for him in the long term. His injuries were simply too extensive. Waldo's family was told to prepare for the worst. In his final moments, there was a nurse seated by his side. She saw a tear roll down his cheek. She was overwhelmed with sadness when she saw it. Tears welled in her eyes as she watched Waldo's final moments. She was deeply moved. The nurse knew Waldo didn't want to die, but his tear showed her he that he was about to. Tears ran down her cheeks. The time had come for Waldo to go. As the tear on his cheek rolled off of his face and dripped onto his pillow, the monitors that were tracking his vital organs went into alarm. Waldo's heart stopped. The nurse sat by him and she cried. She sat there for a long while as the single tone of the alarm rang in her ears. She just stared into nothing for a long time. There was nothing she could do, but she would never forget those last dying moments with Waldo. In the very instant that Waldo passed away, the Silver City and the dragon's light, were also snuffed out. They were like fading candles, that had burned up their last remains of fuel.

The police searched all around Grannies Lane, but they never did work out what may have happened to Waldo. There was a detailed investigation to find the person or persons that may have set Waldo alight and left him for dead, but nothing was ever found. The entire episode remained one of the greatest unsolved mysteries of the nation. Waldo was buried three days later, and his family mourned their loss.

When the Red Dragon returned the Salimandé was most pleased to hear how simple it had been to rid himself of the Maligrandé. He laughed out loud as he finalised his plans to lay siege on the Silver City. First, he would destroy the city, then he would sacrifice the girl. With the balance of evil back in his favour, and both the Silver and Sun city under his control, there was nothing that could stop him. He would mount the next campaign, expanding his empire until it encompassed the entire depth and breadth of Annulus. The Salimandé and his dragon would rule in the darkness of the light of day, and there would be no one to stop them now. He cackled as he patted the Red Dragon in reward for its swift work in ridding them of Waldo.

Another week passed before the advancing army arrived at the Silver City. They quickly surrounded the city's perimeter as they built their camps around it. For another day, they readied themselves for the onslaught to follow. The next day they began. At first, they tried storming the city, but the dome barrier was impenetrable to them. They charged at the dome. It was like smashing into a brick wall. Their bodies were battered and bruised, as they simply bounced off of it. There was no way through for them. Next they tried ramming poles as teams of them raced towards the dome. Again, they bounced off the dome. As they did, they jarred their bodies hard. They gave up. They needed a better way. They re-grouped to re-think their plan of attack.

The next day, the army tried a different approach. They decided to try catapults, so they brought their catapults forward. They set the catapults up so that they could bombard the dome with oil en-flamed rocks. They started the bombardment at first light the next day. The blazing rocks were a frightening sight to everyone inside the city. They could see the burning balls as they came hurtling through the air towards them. The flaming rocks were flung from all directions, and the dome was dotted in red blots as each one hit. The dome glowed at the point of each impact and restored itself, but none came through. It was like a flashing strobe light as the rocks hit and dotted the dome in random fashion. The bombardment never stopped, not even for a moment. At one point, three red hot rocks struck the dome in the exact same place, one after another. The dome resisted the first and then the second rock, but the third rock slipped through. It crashed into one of the houses and blew it to pieces. Waldo's passing had weakened the city's defences.

People in the near vicinity screamed and ran in all directions, as they fled the red hot rock pieces that exploded on impact. It sent red-hot coal debris and burning oil, flying in all directions. The blood-thirsty army outside roared, as the great dome flickered as if it would be snuffed out, but it restored itself and held true. The army's spirits were renewed. At last, the army knew what they had to do to weaken the city's defences. They were filled with renewed enthusiasm. They could taste victory. They aligned their catapults so that they could repeat the successful strike sequence, and in time they managed to adjust their firing to get just a few missiles to break through. Every time a red hot rock crashed through the dome, it caused more carnage as it hit the city below. The city's shield, flickered, restored itself, and held true again.

For two more days, the city was laid under siege and for two days, there was little progress made. The Salimandé was furious and stormed around venting his frustration. He threw a heap of fireballs at those nearest to him. One of the fighters was hit by five balls one after another. He was vaporised on the spot. The Salimandé cackled. The demise of the poor wretch gave him an idea! He got the men to make a huge net. He sent others to fetch more rocks and oil. His plan was to place as many rocks as the dragon could lift. The dragon would next fly above the dome, set the rocks alight, and then drop the rocks on the dome. The falling rocks would create a massive simultaneous impact on the dome. He surmised that most of the burning rocks would smash through. That way, they would be able to destroy great chunks of the city at a time. They might even manage to overload and destroy the city's central defence systems as well. If they did, the city would be theirs for the taking.

With the Salimandé's evil plan in place, the army made haste in its preparations. Even so, it would be another day before the vial horde would be ready for the next assault. The city waited in terrified contemplation. Everyone in the city felt trapped and helpless. They were filled with fear and anxiety, as they waited like sitting ducks, not knowing what would happen next. The people inside the city knew, that whatever was coming next, it wasn't going to be good for them. An eerie silence fell over the city both inside and out, which didn't help the people trapped inside with their uneasiness. The army organised teams of men and sent them out in all directions to bring back more rocks, and more oil, whilst other teams were sent to search for more rope. Those left behind in the camp started the laborious work of making the many nets that they would need.

It had been several weeks since Waldo's charred body had been laid to rest. His remains lay buried in its coffin, deep beneath the earth. Darkness fell over the cemetery where he lay. It was a clear crisp spring night, and the stars shone brightly as the moon crept up from the distant horizon. The full moon was in a very close orbit to the Earth that week. It was bigger and closer than anyone could remember the full moon ever being. The moon shone extremely brightly as it lit up the land. It was a super-moon, a one in a century rarity, but as it turned out, it was incredibly good timing for Waldo. The super-moon's powerful rays bathed the Earth in shining moon light. Waldo's tombstone glistened in the bright light. Inside Waldo's coffin deep below, the blackened scar on Waldo's chest began to glow, ever so faintly at first, and then stronger. As the moon's life-giving forces strengthened they penetrated far beneath the earth. Finally, Waldo's scar was shinning ever so brightly again.

Waldo's lifeless body levitated inside the coffin. The Source of Life re-connected with Waldo once more, so that it could surround his charred corpse in its life-giving forces. It started its work on repairing his damaged cells. For three days and nights, the Source of Life poured massive amounts of life-giving energy back into Waldo's, all but lifeless body. On the third night, Waldo's body was completely healed and rejuvenated. It was time for his organs to be snapped back into life. The Source of Life had managed to place Waldo in a state of suspended animation, just seconds before he was to draw his last dying breath in the hospital. The Source of Life knew that it would need a powerful moon before it could heal the level of damage that the dragon had caused. With what little was left of Waldo's life force suspended, the Source of Life was forced to wait for the next super-moon, before it could firstly heal and then un-suspend him. With the Source's work complete, it was now time to revive Waldo. In an instant, Waldo broke out his suspended state. Waldo woke with a huge gasp of air as he filled his empty lungs with the stale air trapped inside the coffin. He coughed and nearly choked. There was the strong stench of burnt and rotting flesh, and barely enough air to fill his lungs.

Waldo's first thought was, "Where am I?" Using his night vision, he could see the padded arch inside the coffin's lid. He could barely move. He was in pitch black darkness. He reached out in the dark with his arms. He tried to push on the lid of the coffin, but he could barely move his arms. It was too heavy to move anyway. Suddenly, Waldo recalled what the dragon had done to him. He remembered the Red Dragon bearing down on him, and the fireball that engulfed him and burnt him to a crisp. He felt around and the shape of the box he was in. It reminded him of the inside of a coffin. He exclaimed out loud, "A coffin!" It was everyone's worst nightmare—buried alive in a coffin! He must get out of here, but how? He was trapped! Even if he could push the coffin lid open, there were tonnes of dirt above him. He would never be able to get free, but if he didn't get out of the coffin soon, he would run out of air and suffocate.

Waldo's mind raced through all of his options. The solution came to him in a flood of relief. The transgression band he thought. He felt for it. He was exuberant. It was still there! Fortunately, it had been left on his wrist when he was buried. It was charred black and had been burnt into his skin, so even the hospital hadn't removed it as they normally would have. Waldo was in luck! Waldo quickly clasped it. He hoped it would still work "Great Book, help me!" he shouted.

"Oh Waldo, I thought you were lost. When I lost cont . . ."

Waldo cut the Book off abruptly as he ordered, "Get me back—NOW!"

The Book transported Waldo immediately. Waldo found himself standing naked, back in the great domed room beside the Pedestal of Light. The book transported some new clothes onto his body, and then his Maligrandé robe.

The book exclaimed with some urgency, "The city is under siege Waldo. You must hurry. Your people need you!"

Waldo's immediate thoughts were only for Macey. He asked the book, "Where is Macey?"

"She is in the tower," the book replied.

"Transport me there," instructed Waldo.

Waldo shimmered to the tower. Macey was huddling into a corner, sobbing as she faced the wall. Her face was buried in the palms of her hands. Waldo went over to hear and gently brushed the hair from her face. As she turned her face towards him, their eyes met. Macey exclaimed, "Waldo!" She wrapped her arms around him and held him as tightly as she could. She sobbed as she kissed him. He kissed her back. After a long tender moment, they both rejoiced in their relief. They were back together again—at last!

Macey made Waldo promise that he would never leave her like that again. Waldo promised her that he wouldn't. Macey's eyes lit up. She never wanted to be separated from him again. Macey remembering that the city was under attack, exlaimed, "The Salimandé is attacking the city Waldo! They are hurtling burning rocks at the dome. Some have come crashing through, and even though they have stopped for almost a day now, I know that is because something terrible is about to happen. I'm terribly afraid Waldo and . . ."

"Sshhh . . . ," said Waldo soothingly. "Don't worry Macey, I will think of something. Everything is going to be ok now."

Waldo looked out the tower window. He could see the invading army's soldiers were everywhere. It looked grim.

They had the city completely surrounded. He took a moment to think. Soon it would be night fall. Waldo turned to Macey and said, "Macey, I want you to find somewhere safer to hide, and then I want you to wait for me until this is all over . . . do you understand?"

"Yes," replied Macey. She left for the tower stairs and then turned and ran back, throwing her arms around Waldo and kissing him. She held him tight. "Oh Waldo I thought I lost you. I love you so much," she said, as she kissed him again.

Waldo insisted, "Go Macey! We will talk later ok?"

Macey responded, "Ok, later then, but please, be careful Waldo."

Waldo clasped the band, nodding. He started discussing the situation with the Book as Macey left. "It doesn't look too good from here Book. Do you have any ideas?"

The Book computed the strategic options. It responded, "Take away their desire to fight Waldo?"

Waldo replied, "Nice idea. How do we do that?"

"Moon beams Waldo," said the book. "Fill their camp with the same moon beams you used to stop the Salimandé. If there is even a skerrick of good still left in them, it will fill their sad empty hearts, full of the love for life, and their families that they once knew and cherished. If you can reunite them with the desire to be with their families once again, they will lose their desire to continue the fight. "Ok. Let's do it," agreed Waldo.

Waldo waited for night fall, and then, for the moon to rise. It was only a half moon, but Waldo hoped it would be enough. When it was time, the Book said to Waldo, "Concentrate on creating a moon beam Waldo." Waldo concentrated, and after a short time, his body began to lift from the floor. The tower filled with a huge flood of light that poured out of the scar on his chest. Waldo exclaimed, "How about that!"

The Great Book exclaimed in response, "Nice work Waldo! Now all you have to do is get within range, so we can fill their dark souls with light. Hopefully, by tomorrow, the lot of them will be wondering what they are doing here."

Waldo asked, "Can you transport me into their camp Book?"

"Of course," replied the Book.

"Then let us wait until they are asleep," said Waldo.

Waldo waited until it was late in the night. He asked the Great Book to transport him into the camp of sleeping soldiers. The Salimandé and the dragon never slept in the camp for they didn't trust their own murderous horde. They knew, that given the chance, they would not hesitate to slit their throats as they slept. When Waldo arrived in the camp, all he found was sleeping soldiers. In fact, all of them were fast asleep. Such was their confidence that there wouldn't be any attack from within the city, that they didn't even bother to post watches.

Waldo concentrated. His body raised itself into the air until it was five meters above the ground. Waldo then concentrated even harder, as he turned his focus on creating the moon beam. Suddenly, there was a great out pouring of light emanating from the scar on Waldo's chest. It flooded the area in bright light. Waldo moved slowly through the air, directed the moonbeams directly at each and every one of the sleeping soldiers in turn, as he did a complete circle of the city's perimeter. As he did so, some of the soldiers were woken up by the bright light. They stood up looking very confused. After shaking their heads and pausing for a few moments, they packed their belongings, and walked off into the night. Waldo delighted, reported back to the Book excitedly, "Yes Book! It works!"

The moonbeams were like a large spotlight, so it wasn't long before Waldo had spotted every soldier individually with the beam. After he was finished, he got the book to transported him back to the palace. Satisfied with a good nights work, he joined Macey in their chambers, and they slept soundly in each others arms for the rest of the night.

Next morning as the sun rose, the Salimandé and the red dragon returned. When they arrived back at the camp, the soldiers were all still sleeping. Furious at their tardiness, the dragon roared and shot great bursts of flame through the air to awaken them. One by one, the soldiers slowly awoke. They rubbed their weary eyes. They were still tired, but strangely, they felt good about themselves. It was something that they hadn't felt in a very long time. They wondered what they were all doing outside the Silver City, and since no one seemed to know why they were there, they picked themselves up, packed their belongings and left.

The men felt so happy, that they started singing as they dispersed in all different directions. The Salimandé and the dragon were furious. They swooped around shouting commands, and demanding that the soldiers fall back in line. No one cared. None even bothered to listen. When the dragon started to blow great walls of flames directly at the men, it just made things worse. The soldiers fled as fast and as far away as they could. It was pointless. There were simply too many for the Salimandé and the dragon to round up. With the Salimandé's great army gone, the Sliver City was safe once more.

With their entire army now gone, there was nothing left for the Salimandé and the dragon to do, except to skulk back to the City of Gold. There they could re-group and plan their next murderous conquest. As the people of the Silver City watched the Salimandé, and the dragon disappear into the distant horizon, the people cheered loudly and rejoiced. There was dancing in the streets. Waldo had woken Macey early in the morning, so that together, they could go to the tower to watch what would happen when the sun rose. They watched the whole episode unfold before them. Macey was delighted at how clever Waldo, and the Book were. She cuddled him, then smothered him in her complete adoration.

When Waldo and Macey emerged at the main entrance to the palace, they found that the people had again gathered there.

When the people saw the couple, they applauded and cheered, and then they celebrated with dancing in the streets once more. Waldo and Macey joined them. The celebrations carried on, throughout the entire day. Miadrag still slept. In fact, he had slept the whole time the city was under siege, and he continued to sleep, even through all the commotion from the celebrations, that followed.

The next day after a good night's sleep, Waldo and Macey made their way to the Great Hall. There they ate a hearty breakfast, along with several hundred others. As they ate, the Caretaker arrived. When he saw Waldo and Macey, he headed straight over, and took the seat beside Waldo. He began to eat the meal that was placed in front of him, whilst commending Waldo on a job extremely well done. "Once again, you have proven Waldo, that you are the protector of this great city, and indeed, I might hasten to add, this kingdom. You did it Waldo. You saved us . . . well done!" The Caretaker ate some more before he paused again and continued, "Look how the people relish their King Waldo."

Waldo raised his hand, motioning at the Caretaker to stop speaking. "I have made my decision," he said, "And I can see no better time than now to share it with everyone." With that Waldo walked over to the marble podium. He looked out into the room, and the room fell silent as he readied himself to speak. Waldo spoke in a clear loud voice. "Citizens of the Silver City, let us rejoice in our glorious triumph over the evil forces that have tried to destroy us this past week. Let us thank God that we as the people, are again united in the glory of each other, and of this grand kingdom." There were great cheers both from within and outside the palace. The Book was piping video of Waldo's speech, throughout the entire city.

Waldo continued, "People of this great kingdom. I would like to thank you for your warm hospitality, and for your love for Macey and I. We came to you, but a few months ago as strangers, but now you embrace us as a part of your beloved family." There was a great eruption of applause from everywhere. The crowd's roar could be heard from far away. When there was more silence, Waldo continued, "In our time here, we have met every one of you, and we have felt your love for us, and as I stand before you today, I testify to our great love for you, the loyal subjects of this magnificent land." There were even greater cheers and applause, even louder than before.

After the people had quietened once more, he continued, "Even so, there is one thing that remains unanswered. In the words of our good friend the Caretaker, who has for the past month asked me many times the very question, I ask you all now . . ." Waldo paused and allowed the silence for a few seconds before continuing, "I ask you dear people, what is a kingdom that has no king?" There was complete silence. The people waited for Waldo's next words to come with great anticipation. Waldo again allowed the power of a few seconds of silence to settle again. "And so I say, it is time my friends, for us to decide who will be king, and so I ask you all to tell me now, who will you choose to be your king?" There was a great tumultuous roar in response, as all the people in the city replied in unison, "Waldo! Waldo! Waldo!" The roar of the people continued for another minute. It could be heard for kilometres around.

Waldo placed his hands in the air, and the voices both inside, and out fell silent. "If it be your will," continued Waldo, "Then it would be my great honour, to be your King." Suddenly everyone rose from his or her seat, and there was great cheering and loud applause from all around. After the cheering and applause had died down again, Waldo continued, "But before I can become your King, I must ask someone very dear to my heart, a simple question." He turned to Macey and motioned for her to come over to the podium. Macey walked over to Waldo.

Waldo kneeled on one knee, as he took Macey by the hands, and looked deeply into her eyes. As she looked down upon him wide-eyed and smiling, he said, "Macey, you are my one true love. Without you, I am lost and alone. It is with all my love for you, that I ask you in full view of the entire kingdom, to consider this important question." We waited a few seconds as he gathered himself. He then continued, "Macey Sanders, will you do me the very great honour, of being my wife?" The room was still. You could hear a pin drop. There wasn't a dry eye in the city. Tears of anticipation, ran down the cheeks of those waiting anxiously for Macey's reply. Macey smiled at Waldo. Her eyes glistened as she replied, "Waldo, you are the one true love of my life. Without you, I am lost and alone . . . my heart races every time I am near you, and ever since I first met you, I have had no other great desire, but to spend the rest of my life with you. Waldo Middins, my answer is yes! I will gladly be your wife." The whole city erupted in cheers as Waldo took Macey in his arms, and kissed her deeply. The people cheered even more when Macey wrapped her arms around Waldo's neck, and she kissed him passionately back.

Finally, when silence fell again, they looked up to see Miadrag smiling. He exclaimed heartily, "Congratulations Waldo! Congratulations Macey! Three cheers for Waldo and Macey," and the city erupted in cheering again and again. Finally, the Caretaker came over to the podium and said, "People of this great kingdom, let us truly rejoice in this great day. For this day has brought us a true and rightful King, and Queen. It is my great pleasure to proclaim that the royal wedding coronation of our King and Queen of Annulus, will be held in one month from today. He raised his hands high in the air as he said, "Let the preparations, and festivities begin!"

The city erupted once more as Waldo, Macey and the Caretaker returned to their seats. The feasting and festivities continued throughout the day, and then throughout the night and the rest of the week. The next day, the Caretaker came to Macey and Waldo. He presented them with trays full of diamond engagement rings, for them to choose from. Macey picked a beautiful crafted gold and silver ring, with three sparkling blue diamonds in it. As Waldo placed it on Macey's wedding finger, the Caretaker proclaimed that they were now, officially engaged.

Back at the City of Gold, as the Silver City celebrated, the Salimandé and the Red Dragon raged. They ordered even bloodier battles in the great arena, but even then, they squirmed and writhed with rage, flinging fireballs and bursts of flame into the arena, whenever their thoughts drifted back to their humiliating defeat. The City of Gold provided them with many distractions, but as much as they tried to keep their minds from wandering back to their devastating day, they simply couldn't. The events of the Sliver City plagued them. It had failed to quench their unquenchable thirst for death and destruction, and they had lost an entire army as well. How could this happen? It just raised so many nagging questions that needed to be answered. For one thing, they still didn't know why their murderous horde deserted them.

When finally, word came back that Waldo, was in fact, very much alive, and that he would soon marry Macey, the Salimandé was in such a rage that he summoned the Red Dragon to come at once. When the Red Dragon arrived, the Salimandé scolded the dragon, and he damned his incompetence. He ranted and raved for a very long time. As he raved on and on, the Salimandé got madder and madder, until finally he had worked himself up so much, that he let go with a flurry of fireballs, that hit and severely wounded the dragon. One of them nearly blew off one of the dragon's wings. The Red Dragon was furious at this outrage. He blew a great burst of flames at the Salimandé, who was caught off guard by the dragon's impudence. The Salimandé was incinerated, just as Waldo was. The dragon limped away leaving the Salimandé smouldering on the floor. The Salimandé's eyes glowed a dull red. He would need all of his remaining strength, in order to heal himself.

When the word spread of the demise of the Salimandé and his dragon, the evil clans within the City of Gold, wasted no time in starting their looting and plundering. They took everything they could lay their hands on, especially the external gold plating sheets, that lined the city's exterior. When they were finished plundering, all that was left of the great City of Gold, was a cold grey city of stone. It would shine no more. It was now a desolate place. The Salimandé and the dragon, dragged themselves hastily to their secret hideaways. They needed to set about the lengthy business of healing themselves, before it was too late, and they would use every bit of their last energy reserves to do so. It wasn't going to be easy, as their injuries were massive, but they knew if they were found in this condition, they would not be able to defend themselves. Indeed if found, they would be quickly dispatched by the vagabonds in the city, who would relish the opportunity to be rid of them both, once and for all. Safe in their respective hideaways, they continued the long process of healing their devastating, self-inflicted wounds. It was only a few days later, that the city was completely deserted. The City of Gold was now nothing more, than a deserted cold stone relic.

The greed driven vermin who had come to plunder the city's gold, now plundered it at will. They then scurried off with their booty. Dotted across the land, far and wide, there were black hooded figures carrying great sacks of gold, over their shoulders. They struggled to carry the heavy sacks in their haste to be as far away as possible, before they were caught. They knew they needed to hurry. If they were caught by the Red Dragon, or the Salimandé, it would mean certain death. They made haste. In no time at all, they found the means to transport themselves to different worlds, were they knew they would be safe again. All of them disappeared, all of them, without trace.

The Salimandé and the Red Dragon, were now lords over nothing, and no one. They were enraged at each other, for each other's' insolence, and the brutality they had exacted upon each other. Their hatred for each other was now intense. They knew, if they were to meet again, there would be a vicious fight. A fight that would not end until one or both were dead. To top things off, with the demise of the city and its inhabitants, there was no evil left on Annulus for them to rule, so Annulus was no longer suitable for their evil purposes. The Salimandé and the Red Dragon left Annulus, both searching the galaxies for new places of evil for them to reside in and lord over. There they would re-group. In time, they would re-build their evil empires, and then they would exact their revenge.

It was a great day, for all of creation. It was an unexpected turn of events. The balance of evil, took a severe blow. All things good rejoiced! When the word of the demise of the City of Gold, the Salimandé, and the Red Dragon reached the Silver City, there were even more reasons to celebrate. At last, Annulus was free of evil altogether! No longer would the village people have to live in fear of being plundered and slaughtered, as murderous hoards passed through their lands, burning everything in their path to the ground. It was finally over. Annulus was at peace at last!

The Coronation of Love

he Silver City was in a frenzy. Everyone darted here and there, as they went about preparing for the great day, now just weeks away. Streets were being decorated. Proceedings were being planned. Feasts and festivities were being organised. The hive of activity was unrelenting. There was so much to do, and very little time to do it in. The palace sent out official messengers to all corners of the land, to announce the great union between Waldo and Macey. They did so with loud trumpeting and much fan-fare as they entered each village. Macey's entire village travelled to the Silver City so that they could attend the wedding coronation. The city embraced them, and insisted that they be provided with permanent homes so that they could remain within the city and be near Macey. Macey's parents accepted permanent residence in the palace, which was only fitting, as very soon they would become The Queen Father, and The Queen Mother of Annulus.

Waldo and Macey, were according to the laws of the kingdom, forbidden from seeing each other for the entire month leading up to their wedding. They were given quarters in different wings of the palace, so that they wouldn't bump into each other by accident. The only way they could communicate with each other, was to write each other letters. The letters were delivered by aids. Waldo and Macey wrote to each other profusely. They wrote of their loneliness, and of their undying love for each other. They both wanted the month to go by quickly. Both waited in excited anticipated of the day they would finally be married. They would then be together, for the rest of their lives.

As it turned out, the two were kept busy enough. There were dresses to pick and ceremonial words to practice and learn. When Waldo wasn't writing Macey letters, or being attended to for the wedding coronation, he would clasp his wrist and talk with the Great Book. Waldo and the Book became good friends. Waldo loved to hear the many stories that the Book told. Through its stories, the Book taught Waldo, all about the great empires that had come and gone, and of how other successful kings had ruled.

When Waldo had learnt enough about other worlds, and of other successful kingdoms, he enquired about the Maligrandé. The Great Book told Waldo the legend of the Maligrandé was first foretold millions of years ago. There had been no recording of a Maligrandé ever existing before Waldo. This did not mean there had never been a Maligrandé in the past. It did mean, however, no-one actually knew what a Maligrandé's powers were capable of. The Book explained that the Source of Life was a very significant piece in the legend. The Source of Life, is the life force that is formed from the combined four elements of Earth, Water, Fire and Air. Legend tells us, the Maligrandé, as you are Waldo, will be born a Virgo, the earth sign of purity and righteousness, in a year of the Water Dragon. These elements combined with the Fire and Air elements of the Moon Dragon complete a full circle of elements. This is what is needed to draw from the power, that is within the Source of Life itself.

The Book went on to explain to Waldo, that he can command the elements of Fire, Air, Earth and Water, just as the Source of Life does. It follows then, continued the Book, that when you command the Fire sign, fire being a type of light, you can conjure moonbeams, moon light, moon vision, moonballs and even fire itself. Taking command of an Earth sign will give you earthly powers from within the soul, such as healing, nurturing, fairness, righteousness, growth, intuition and thinking. Commanding the Air sign will leverage powers of the air such as telepathy, levitation, give control over wind, and the ability to move objects through thought, and so on. Commanding the Water sign you could theoretically, part a sea, create rain, breathe under water and so forth.

Waldo had already discovered some of his powers, but there would be many other combinations that he would discover in time. The book went on to explain that Waldo could create virtually anything he wished, by manipulating multiple elements in various amounts, at the same time. The book continued to explain that he could in theory create a thunderstorm using the correct combinations of air, fire and water, for instance, just as the Source of Life in nature does. The book finished by telling Waldo that his gifts would require imagination to discover, and then practice to master, but when sufficiently skilled, virtually anything was possible.

At that moment, the Caretaker happened along. "Oh there you are Waldo. I've been looking all over the palace for you. Come, it is time for your robes to be fitted."

"Off you go then," chuckled the Book, "Can't have you looking sloppy on the big day can we?" Waldo left the Dome Room with the Caretaker and was fitted with his ceremonial garments. There were only a few weeks to go, so they were in a dither. They were worrying that they may not be able to get all the robes finished in time.

Waldo missed Macey very much. He yearned to see her beautiful face, and her perfect smile again. Finally, they were both summoned to the palace abbey to practice their wedding and coronation vows. Everyone was fussing about. Waldo and Macey looked at each other lovingly. Macey moved to embrace

Waldo. She was stopped by her assistants and reminded that this wasn't permitted until after the wedding. Their hearts throbbed as they yearned to reach out and touch each other. Waldo and Macey practiced their vows for an hour. It was time they cherished together, very much. The session finished. Waldo and Macey were separated again.

Time as it turned out, did in fact, pass quickly. Before Waldo and Macey knew it, the great day had arrived. The entire population lined the streets to celebrate. They were anxious to catch a glimpse of the handsome couple as they passed by on parade. Waldo and Macey paraded the streets at different times in two separate carriages. The carriages were vivid white, open-air carriages. They were elaborately decorated with the Maligrandé symbols embossed in sliver on their doors. Four magnificent white stallions drew each carriage. Waldo's carriage left first, so that he would arrive at the Abbey before Macey. Macey's carriage would leave afterwards, so that she would arrive at the Abbey after Waldo had sufficient time to enter the Abbey, and be waiting for her at the alter.

Macey looked absolutely stunning! She wore a short-sleeved white satin-hooped dress, that was cut short at the shoulder to reveal her beautiful neckline. It formed a modest V shape in front of her stunning figure. It was elaborately embroidered with silver and gold patterns of subtle criss-crosses inside silver outlines. It combined loops and straight lines to complete a master-piece of timeless elegance in what was a wondrously beautifully and most tastefully decorated piece. It was a wedding dress, indeed fit for a Queen.

To accompany the dress Macey wore white gloves that finished above the elbow, and her hair was long and flowing. Her face was covered by a delicately embroidered matching gold and silver veil, that covered her face and neck, as it hung down past her shoulders. Macey's train was snow-white velvet, with leaves in the middle panel that boarded the main inner panel. Inside the bordered panel, was embroidered the emblem of the Maligrandé in silver, wrapped in swirls of magnificently decorative trimmings. The edges of the train were soft white fur, sparsely dotted with black flecks. The train had a spotted fur collar that stood straight up, and it was tied around Macey's neck with matching silver tassels.

Waldo looked grand in his royal robes. He wore a long white satin jacket and vest, embroidered with gold and silver patterns. The jacket had silver gilded cuffs. He wore white trousers with shiny black knee-high boots. Waldo also wore a cloak that was identical to Macey's in design, with a stiff upright spotted fur collar that tied around his neck with matching silver tassels. As the respective carriages passed by, the people lining the streets went crazy with excitement, waving and cheering loudly. They threw rose petals in the air. It was a perfect day, with clear blue skies, and a warm sun that shone brightly in the noon sky. Everyone beamed with happiness and jubilation. It was indeed a joyous day!

After completing his parade through the streets encircling the city, Waldo arrived back at the palace. He made his way to the grand abbey where the wedding ceremony and coronation would soon take place. As Waldo walked into the abbey, the strings Orchestra began to play "Joy of Man's Desiring" and the air was filled with a mixture of calm excitement, and anxious anticipation. Miadrag was waiting for Waldo inside the abbey. He gave Waldo a sly wink as Waldo entered the abbey, and walked down the aisle to the altar at the opposite end. As Waldo waited, the palace Cardinals dressed in their full ceremonial dress, quietly went about making their final preparations, in readiness for Macey's arrival. The abbey was a mass of colour and gaiety, and it was adorned with the most exquisite flower arrangements, and all forms of finery.

Waldo waited patiently for what seemed like an eternity. Suddenly, the orchestra started to play "Arrival of the Queen of Sheba" as it heralded Macey's arrival outside. The air was filled with excitement and expectation. As Waldo turned he saw

Macey and her father come through the entrance to the abbey. Macey looked up at Waldo, and he could see her sparkling smile beneath her veil. Waldo, who was always taken aback by her beauty, was completely stunned by it now. As Macey and her father waited at the entrance, Macey's helpers readied her for her walk down the aisle. Macey linked arms with her father as they readied themselves. She couldn't stop smiling. She was truly happy, and it showed.

The orchestra was silent for a moment, and then, after allowing a short time of complete silence, it started playing joyously, "The Wedding March" with overtures of flute that rang out to the sheer delight of its listeners. Macey's father, led his beloved daughter, ever so slowly down the aisle, as the orchestra played flawlessly. Macey and Waldo both stared into each other's eyes, as they smiled at each other intently from afar. Macey's father grinned the entire time. He savoured this deeply special, and very proud moment. When finally, they arrived at the altar, Macey's father handed Macey over to Waldo, and took his seat. Waldo and Macey linked arms as they both stepped forward. They walked a short distance, and stopped before the High Cardinal, who was now waiting patiently, and smiling back at them. When Waldo and Macey were finally in position, the Cardinal began the wedding ceremony.

Macey and Waldo were filled with joy and happiness. It was a powerful moment for them, and they soaked up the tremendous atmosphere in the beautifully ornate, and superbly decorated cathedral. The proceedings were dotted with much pomp and ceremony. There were many songs sung by the choir. The congregation joined in. The singing of the entire city rang out across the land. These were precious moments for Macey and Waldo, and the time passed by too quickly for the young couple, as it didn't seem to them long at all, before the Cardinal asked Macey and Waldo to face each other. As they stood side on to the congregation, he asked them to take each other's hands. They turned and looked into each other's eyes, as they stood hand in hand, facing each other.

The Cardinal then said, "Waldo Middens, as you stand here before God today, will you take Macey Sanders, to be your lawfully wedded wife, to love her, and to cherish her, in sickness and in health, for richer or poorer, from this day forward, until death you do part?" Waldo replied as he looked deeply into Macey's eyes, "Macey, you are my one true love. Without you, my life is empty and my soul is lost. So let it be known throughout this land, that I, Waldo Middens, will take you Macey Sanders, with all of my heart, to be my lawfully wedded wife. I will love you and cherish you, in sickness and in health, for richer or poorer, from this day forward, until death do us part."

The cardinal turned to Macey and said, "Macey Sanders as you stand here before God today, will you take Waldo Middins, to be your lawfully wedded husband, to love him and to cherish him, in sickness and in health, for richer or poorer, from this day forward, until death do you part?" Macey replied as she looked deeply into Waldo's eyes, "Waldo, you are my one true love. Without you, my life is empty and my soul is lost. So let it be known throughout this land, that I, Macey Sanders will take you Waldo Middins, with all of my heart, to be my lawfully wedded husband. I will love you and cherish you, in sickness and in health, for richer or poorer, from this day forward, until death do us part."

The Cardinal asked for the rings, and the ring bearer bought them forward on a white velvet cushion with silver tassels. Waldo took Macey's ring, and as he slowly slipped it onto her wedding finger, he said, "With this ring, I thee wed." Macey took Waldo's ring, and as she slipped it gently onto Waldo's wedding finger she said, "And with this ring, I thee wed."

The cardinal then said, "With the powers invested in me, as we stand here today in the witness of God, and in the presence of this great gathering, I now pronounce you, husband and wife. Waldo, you may now kiss your bride."

Waldo lifted Macey's veil. Oh, she was beautiful. They brought their eager lips together, and they kissed passionately as their repressed love for each other poured out. The entire congregation and the crowds outside, cheered in a tremendous roar. After some time, upon finishing their lengthy embrace, they turned to the congregation. They raised their held hands high, in triumph. It was indeed a day to celebrate their great victory. The crowds felt it too, and the crowds went wild!

When the cheers had died down, the coronation ceremony began. Waldo and Macey took their vows to the kingdom and its people, and after much ado, the cardinal placed, firstly, the King's crown on Waldo's head, and then the Queen's crown on Macey's head. He proclaimed, "I now pronounce you, King and Queen of Annulus."

The roars were deafening. There was much celebration in the streets. Rose petals filled the air and the orchestra played joyously, "There is Love." Waldo and Macey walked back down the aisle and made their way out of the abbey, and into the open carriage that Macey had arrived in. The carriage jolted as it moved forward. Waldo and Macey paraded merrily through the streets once more. The people waved flags and cheered, and as they passed by, they showered Waldo and Macey in rose petals and rice as they smiled and waved back to them.

After the parade of the new King and Queen, there was a magnificient feast in the great hall. The two ate heartily, and they danced throughout the night as the orchestra played, and the people celebrated. Miadrag's heart was full of gladness. He couldn't believe that he had not only managed to find a Maligrandé and fitting King, but a fitting Queen for Annulus as well. "It doesn't get better than this," he said to himself. Miadrag rejoiced. He could see that the new king and queen were loved greatly by the people. They were such a handsome couple too.

Macey never stopped smiling. She looked so beautiful, and Waldo very handsome. They danced and laughed, and held each other in their arms. Their love for each overcame them, and they kissed, and they kissed, and they kissed some more; much to the delight of their guests. The celebrations went on and on, late into the night, until finally it was time for the newly weds to leave the wedding party. Waldo and Macey said their good-byes and departed. They retired to the royal honeymoon suite.

The Caretaker took them to their suite, bid them good night and left them outside the closed door. Waldo opened the door, picked Macey up in his arms and carried her over the threshold as they kissed passionately. He carried her over to the bed where he laid her down gently, and kissed her some more. Macey kissed him passionately back, and the lovers were overwhelmed with their great love for each other, and the fire of passion rose within them. Finally, tired and exhausted from the greatest day of their lives, they fell asleep in each other's arms, and they slept until late, the following morning.

In the morning as the sun was shining brightly through the windows, that overlooked the great expanse of the country, beyond the city, there was a polite knock at the door. After a short time, the door opened. There was the clatter of a food trolley being wheeled into the room. It was one of the maids who as she entered, chirpily announced, "Breakfast is served your highnesses." The maid served them breakfast in bed, and then left them. It was an exquisite meal, prepared especially by the head chef.

After breakfast, Waldo and Macey slipped into the spa bath, that was in one of the adjoining rooms. They sipped on the cool exotic fruit juices they had been brought for breakfast. They kissed and played in the bubbling water of the spa. When they were done playing, they got dressed and sat by the window, re-living their glorious days before the wedding, and then the great day itself. They had a lot to catch up on. They talked and talked.

When they were done talking, Macey ran over and jumped into the bed. She motioned Waldo to join her, so he hopped into bed, and kissed her. She kissed him passionately back. Very soon, they were overcome once more, with the fiery passion they shared for each other.

For the next three days, the couple's meals were served in their suite, as they enjoyed each other's company. The time that they spent together in these early days, just the two of them, made the bonds between them grow stronger and stronger. They shared many intimate moments together as they explored each other's minds, their souls, and their bodies. Life for Waldo and Macey as a couple, was simply perfect!

It was on the evening of the third day, that the Caretaker knocked cautiously on their door, and sought permission to enter. The Caretaker entered, after he heard the voices within respond, "Come in." Macey and Waldo were sitting at their table by the window chatting as he entered. "Your highnesses, we have planned for you a surprise honeymoon, so if it pleases you, I will make arrangements for your transport in the morning."

Macey, overcome with excitement, exclaimed "A surprise honeymoon Waldo!"

Waldo asked, "When do we leave Caretaker?"

"I'll meet you at the Pedestal of Light at ten in the morning," replied the Caretaker. He bid them a good evening and left.

Macey and Waldo's imaginations went wild as they tried to guess what their surprise destination might be. Waldo couldn't help notice how beautiful Macey was and how alive she was when she got excited, so he kissed her, and she kissed him back, and then they kissed some more. Waldo picked Macey up and carried her over to the bed, and before they knew it, they were overwhelmed with passion once again. In the morning, after breakfast, they slipped into the spa bath once more. When they were done they dressed, and made their way to the domed room that housed the Great Book and the Pedestal of Light. When they arrived, the Caretaker was waiting for them. He had a big smile on his face. "Ah there you are," he said. Macey and Waldo greeted the Caretaker with excited expectations.

The Caretaker explained to Macey that in order to transport her, she would need a transgression band. He asked her to stand in front of The Great Book, and place a hand on each page. Macey walked over to the Book, and placed her left hand on the left page and her right hand on the right page of the open book. As she did so, The Book glowed, and a crystal transgression band appeared on her wrist. For the first time, she heard the calm soothing voice of The Great Book inside her head say, "Macey, as long as you wear this band, whenever you activate it, you will be able to talk with me, no matter where you are. To activate the band, all you need to do is clasp it with your other hand. The band is designed so it should never need to come off Macey, but if it is removed, you will no longer be able to talk with me, and I won't be able to track or transport you."

Macey asked, "How is this happening? I mean . . . I can hear and speak to you with my mind."

"Yes Macey, placing your hands on my open pages or activating the band will enable you to speak with me. When you and Waldo are ready, all you need to do is activate your bands, and I will transport you to your honeymoon destination." Macey stepped back from The Book, and it stopped glowing.

Macey exclaimed excitedly, "Waldo, I can speak with The Book. It was just as you explained it to me!" Waldo smiled. The Caretaker explained how he had taken the liberty of packing some travel bags, and had forwarded them to their suite at their tropical paradise destination, on the planet of Nemii. The Caretaker explained that Nemii was a planet with two suns, each with twin moons, which are so perfectly aligned, the entire planet has only one perfect season all year round. Macey looked excited. "Let's go Waldo," she said. They both clasped their crystal bracelets, and were instantly transported to the tropical planet of Nemii.

The Honeymoon Surprise

n arrival at the planet of Nemii, Waldo and Macey were standing at the edge of a magnificent blue lagoon. The lagoon was full of stepped waterfalls that channelled the water flow in various directions. In front of them stood a large carved crystal sign that said, "Welcome to the Crystal Lagoon Resort of Nemii." The resort itself, was in the middle of the blue lagoon. It stood on top of a massive base structure carved out of pure crystal, one hundred meters square and ten meters high. There were four majestic waterfalls that poured from above the four faces of the enormous carved crystal base. The water pouring out from the top of its four faces made it difficult to see the crystal sides of the base underneath. They were hidden by beards of foaming white water pouring over them. On top on this square crystal foundation there were carved great ribbed crystal arches, with perfectly sharp lines and bevels, that formed the columns of the second-level of foundations. The arches supported a third much larger solid crystal base plate. On this third-level crystal foundation plate, the resort building, itself reached upward into the sky—it was a truly magnificent sight!

The resort itself rose in layer after layer of perfectly symmetrical hexagonal crystal spires. The spires were twenty meters in width, and they reached high into the sky. Within each crystal spire, there were hexagonal windows that were aligned, such that they clearly defined twenty separate levels. It was overwhelming in its beauty and its magnificence. The whole resort sparkled in the light of the twin suns. As the sun's rays passed through the crystal of the resort, the light was split into spectrums of light. The reflected rainbow coloured light splashed out over the grounds surrounding the resort. Waldo and Macey just stood there utterly stunned. They had never seen, a more amazing sight.

After a few moments, the resort manager appeared. He literally just appeared right in front of them. He rushed over to greet them. "Waldo, Macey, welcome to our beautiful resort," he said. "Now you don't have to worry about a thing. Your suite has been prepared and is waiting for you. Just follow me, and we will have you settled in, in no time at all." Waldo and Macey followed him. They had made but a few steps before all three of them shimmered and disappeared. The next thing Macey and Waldo knew, they were in the foyer of the resort with the manager explaining all the facilities that the resort offered.

He gave Waldo a hexagonal crystal key, and escorted them to an arched alcove inscribed Honeymoon Suite on top of it. Just stand in here and you will be taken to your room he said. Waldo and Macey walked into the Alcove, and as soon as they were ready pressed the crystal button inside. They were immediately transported. They were stunned when they found themselves standing in a similar alcove, in the foyer outside of their suite. Waldo took the crystal key, and placed it in the hexagonal hole in the wall, just beside the doorway of the honeymoon suite. The door slid open, and the two entered. Their mouths wide open as they gazed at what presented before them. It was absolutely amazing.

Inside their suite, there were a number of large rooms. The walls, the floors, everything . . . was carved into the perfect crystal. Even the furniture was made of crystal. Everything looked pristine with its sharp clear lines. The perfectly polished crystal lustre and shine gave the suite an amazingly clear-clean feel to it. There were several ornately carved crystal vases sitting on the bedside and dining tables. They were filled with colourful exotic flowers, that wafted pleasantly sweet perfumes into the room. Waldo and Macey had never seen anything like this before. The suite had a massive bedroom with a magnificent crystal bed. The bed head was made of ornately carved crystal spires. It matched the resorts' profile. It had a white bed cover with a magnificently embroidered picture of the Crystal Lagoon Resort on it, as well as matching bed linen. There was also a crystal en-suite with double showers, crystal fittings and railings, a huge bubbling spa bath and even crystal toilet bowls and crystal bidet.

Clearly, the suite had everything that they might ever have wished for. The suite took up the very top level of the resort, and from the windows, the views were spectacular. The entire resort was built right on the edge of a secluded bay with pristine white beaches, and clear glistening blue seas. Macey was excited. She had never seen the sea or a beach before. She marvelled at the white capped waves as the surf crashed onto the sandy shore. Across the bay was a beautiful island with jagged mountain tops that gave off a blue-green hue, in the distance. The grassed areas in front of them were a bright green, and there were palms and other exotic tropical plants that provided a perfect balance of colour and greenery. This was a truly beautiful place.

Macey, her voice full of excitement said, "Look Waldo, blue water, have you ever seen anything like it before?" Waldo explained that it was the sea, and that the blue was from the reflection from the sky. "Let's go swimming," replied Macey, even more excited. She rummaged through their bags, but she couldn't find anything to wear. Waldo helped her. He found a bikini for Macey, and some bathers for himself. As he passed the bikini to Macey, he suggested, "Here, try these on." Waldo changed into his bathers as Macey pondered on how a bikini is worn. Waldo helped her with it. Once she had it on, she looked absolutely stunning in it. They grabbed some towels, and went to the beach where they bathed in the sea, and played in the surf for the rest of the day.

That night after they had showered, they found the clothes that had been packed for them in the crystal walk in robe. It was through a doorway to the left of the crystal bed. They dressed lavishly for the evening, and then made their way to the Crystal Dining room. It was another magnificent crystal room. There was an orchestra playing on crystal instruments. Waldo and Macey ate exquisite dishes that they selected from the stunning menu. After they ate, they danced. Waldo held Macey close to him, and Macey snuggled her head into his shoulder. "This is the most perfect time I have ever had in my life," she said. Waldo smiled at her and replied, "I still can't believe its all happening." After they had finished dancing Waldo and Macey returned to their room where they had a long spa, whilst they talked and stared into each other's eyes lovingly. They kissed as they played together in the spa, then they retired to their bed, where they fell fast asleep, quite exhausted.

The following morning, the twin suns rose up in the most spectacular of dawns that one could ever imagine. The skies were filled with spectrums of colour as the suns' rays reached out in spears of brilliantly painted light. It was a tapestry of colour as the light-spears peeled outward in a dance of swords, which sliced the sky and the seas. When the suns' rays hit the Crystal Resort, even more spectrums of light were launched out across the land and towards the sea before it. It was a truly stunning time of day and breath takingly beautiful.

As the suns rose higher in the morning sky, deep prisms of colour sent rainbows of light into the air and across the land. Combined with the magnificence of the heavens above, it was such a striking sight. No soul could help being breathless on seeing such magnificence. As the suns rose higher in the dawn skies, the seas turned from reds, pinks, purples, yellows and to the first faint hues of green and blue. The two lovers' shadowy silhouettes could be seen in the distant window embracing and kissing each other with a passion that swelled in a raging fire within them. Everyone who saw them, couldn't help, but feel their deep love for each other. Indeed there had been no other time throughout their lives, that they had ever felt as content and completely fulfilled, as they did now.

After breakfast, Macey wanted to walk along the beach, so Waldo and Macey walked down to the sea's shore. As they walked, the waves crashed against the shore and ran up the white sandy beach in continuously thinning streams. The streams scampered forward, until eventually they were so thin that they were totally absorbed by the sand. The water completely disappeared beneath the sand, only to be replaced by the next wave as it repeated the cycle. Macey was excited as usual. She found some of the most beautiful seashells that Waldo had ever seen. As Macey raced ahead and picked up shells, and brought them back excitedly to show Waldo, she exuded such happiness. Her face lit up, and her eyes sparkled like diamonds.

Waldo melted every time he saw Macey's beautiful smile, and she had a sheer gracefulness about her. The wind caught her hair in flowing streams as she ran towards him, it framed a most magnificent picture of her. Waldo literally lost his breath. He was overcome by her stunning beauty. Waldo couldn't help but feel how lucky he was to have found her. So pure of heart, innocent and sweet, not a bad thought ever entered her mind, and a smile that lit the daytime itself. He smiled to himself, as he contemplated how wonderful, the rest of their lives together will be.

The suns were high in the sky now. The sun's light was extremely bright, so you needed to take care not to look into them or risk seriously damaging your eyes. Macey had raced up the beach and was bending down picking up some sea shells. Waldo's heart began pounding inside his chest. He couldn't believe his ears. It was a sound that ran shivers all through his body. He was frozen with both fear and anguish. It was the whooshing sound of dragon's wings. As his heart was filled with disbelief of what might be about to happen, he was overcome with anxiety A sickening feeling filled his stomach. There was again no time to act.

Waldo looked up and could see the dark shadow of the Red Dragon looming down on them. It emerged from out of the bright light of the suns. Waldo screamed, "Maceeeey, watch out!" Macey stood up. It was too late. Waldo could do nothing but watch helplessly. The Red Dragon was already upon her. As Macey stood up and looked over to Waldo, in the same instant, the Red Ragon was upon her. It picked her up in its sharp claws, and flew away with her kicking and screaming. Waldo threw a flurry of moonballs after the dragon, but the Dragon was too fast. It ducked and weaved so that all the moonballs missed. Waldo was in extreme distress, and he screamed out loud, "Arrrghhhh!!!" He started to run along the beach after them. He just wanted to fly after them now, and rescue Macey. It was all he could think of. He ran as fast as he could, and leapt into the air.

His body rose, as it flew through the air. He lay horizontal with his arms stretched out before him. He found he could steer himself this way as he headed off after the dragon. He was now flying at great speed. Waldo didn't have time to wonder how he was doing this. He was squarely focused on catching up with the dragon and rescuing Macey. The dragon was flying as fast as it could as well. Waldo threw moonballs, and the dragon ducked and weaved in clumsy manoeuvres, as it heaved its heavy body to and fro, in the air to be missed by them. Waldo concentrated on flying faster, and his speed increased until he was travelling so fast, that he had to slow himself down, or he would overtake the dragon. The Dragon somewhat stunned to see Waldo right on his tail, turned and blew fire at Waldo. Waldo dodged and promptly threw another moonball. It hit the dragon fairly and squarely in the middle of its back.

The dragon paralysed by the direct hit, buffeted in the air and then fell with its legs pointing skyward. As the dragon struggled to right its self, it let go of Macey. Macey immediately began plummeting towards the sea below. Waldo dived to catch her before she hit the water. Waldo was just in time, and he managed to catch her in his arms just seconds before she did. Meanwhile, the dragon dropped a short distance more before it regained the use of its wings again. It managed to right itself, and quickly flew off to safety. Waldo didn't see where it had gone. His focus was on Macey. Waldo flew Macey back to the beach where he laid her on some soft green grass nearby. She was unconscious.

Waldo removed his hands from around her body. His clothes were covered in blood. Macey had deep wounds, where the sharp grip of the dragon's claws, had cut her body very badly. Waldo immediately began healing her. He kept repeating out loud, "Hang in their Macey, just hang in there. I am here, and I am going to heal you, just hold on." The tears rolled down Waldo's cheek as he was overcome with grief. He was so afraid that this time, he really was going to lose her. Waldo set to work quickly. He healed first one wound, and then another, until finally, he was done. He picked her up off the ground. He pulled her limp body to his. As he looked intently into her face and stroked her hair, he held her close to him in his arms. His tears fell as his heart burst with sorrow and his fear for Macey's life. Macey was still unconscious in his arms. "Wake up Macey! Wake Up!" he repeated. "Oh please Macey, don't die, oh please God, don't let her die," he cried out loud.

Macey's eyelids twitched and flickered, then slowly they opened. "Oh Macey," Waldo wailed, "Oh thank you God. Thank you, thank you, thank you!"

Waldo asked, "Oh Macey, are you alright?"

Macey smiled back at him and said, "Oh Waldo," as she gave him a cheeky smile. "Oh my hero," she teased as she raised her hand and caressed his face. Waldo kissed her, and she kissed him back.

As Waldo stared into Macey's eyes, she smiled back at him with a most adoring smile. Her eyes were dreamy as she stroked his face with her warm soft hands, and Waldo was overcome by her utter love for him.

As Waldo and Macey embraced each other on the grassy hill, they were so absorbed with each other that they didn't even see the Red Dragon's return. The dragon had again used the sun to shield its approach, and before they knew it, it was upon them. It was horrible. In one heart beat, Waldo was looking deeply into Macey's loving eyes as she smiled back at him, and in the very next heartbeat, he was holding a charred skeleton with jawbone and large teeth exposed as burnt flesh hung off of it. Waldo screamed out at the top of his voice, "Arrrrrrgggghhhhh!"

Macey woke up. "Waldo what's wrong?" She cried out. Waldo was awake. His body was soaked in sweat.

"It was the Red Dragon," he said, "I had a nightmare about the Red Dragon."

"It's ok Waldo. You are safe now. You are here with me, safe in bed, and you are fine. It was just a bad dream that's all," comforted Macey. She pulled him to her bosom and stroked him as she rocked him gently.

"Oh, it was so real," he quivered.

Déjà Vu

It was still the middle of the night and there were four moons shining brightly through the hexagonal windows. Their light force comforted Waldo. Waldo walked to the window where he stood and savoured the bright moon lit night. He mused at the quad trails the moons cut across the sea's waters. The sea glistened as its ripples reflected the moonlight. He relaxed as he drew comfort from the sparkles glistening across the sea. Waldo reassured himself. Even if the Red Dragon were to return, it would be unlikely to do so in such bright moonlight, especially with the four moons out. Waldo returned to the bed, where he cuddled Macey and fell asleep in the warmth of her soothing arms.

The next morning Waldo and Macey woke up with the dawn, and as they watched the magnificent colours and the rainbows of light that came with the rising of the twin suns, Waldo couldn't help being overcome by a feeling of déjà vu. This was just like his dream! Then as they stood at the window, and Macey took him in her arms and kissed him, Waldo was overcome with a frightening reality. His dream was coming true! Waldo tried to hide his anxiety, but when Macey said that she wanted to go for a walk along the beach, he could no longer contain himself. Waldo broke into a sweat, and his face looked as if he had just seen a ghost.

Macey questioned, "What's wrong Waldo?"

"It's the dream," Waldo replied. "This is exactly how the dream started."

"Oh Waldo, don't be silly, it was just a dream. Come let's have breakfast," she said thinking that this would take his mind off of things. She took him by the hand and led him to the Grand Dining room. Waldo calmed down. He was comforted by the thought that breakfast had not been a part of his nightmare. Waldo and Macey enjoyed an exquisite breakfast, and as Waldo relaxed he finally allowed himself to enjoy the moment.

After breakfast, they walked down to the beach. As they walked arm in arm, Macey rested her head on Waldo's shoulder. After a while, Macey noticed some seashells, and she got very excited and raced ahead to pick them up. Waldo was on the look-out, with a growing nervousness. He kept a close eye on the suns to make sure that there were no dark objects flying out of them. He even went for a short run and took a leap into the air, only to fall flat on his face in the wet sand. Macey laughed at him and asked, "What do you think you are doing?"

"Eh, actually I was seeing if I could fly," he replied quite embarrassed.

"Oh, OK then," Macey laughed, "Sometimes you are a strange one Waldo Middins," as she ran around in circles with her arms outstretched pretending to be a bird gliding through the air as she mocked him, laughing the whole time.

Waldo smiled as he checked the sun for any looming danger. His heart stopped! There it was—a dark shadow was looming down on them! He cried out, "Macey it's the dragon!" as he pointed to the black dot growing bigger as it swooped down in their general direction. This time the element of surprise was gone, and Waldo was ready. His arms were a flurry of activity as he filled the air with moonballs. The Dragon ducked and weaved as the first balls missed him, but Waldo had launched them in a pattern that was sure to strike true, even if the dragon dodged and weaved, and hit the dragon, he did.

The dragon was stunned by Waldo's fierce attack. Badly wounded, it fell from the sky. Waldo sent a moonbeam, which he enveloped the falling dragon in, as it fell. The dragon shrivelled and squirmed as it fell straight down. It fell further and further, until it hit the water with a tremendous splash. The dead weight of the dragon hitting the water caused the dragon to go straight down underneath the sea's surface, sending large waves crashing against the shore. The dragon fell deep below with the force of its fall. It was quite some time before its body stopped sinking, and began floating back to the surface again. Finally, the dragon's lifeless body broke the surface. It appeared ever so gently, and then simply bobbed up and down in the sea. Could it be dead, thought Waldo? Certainly, it looked dead!

Waldo knew this dragon may just be pretending to be dead, it was just its style, so just to make sure, he threw moonball after moonball at the dragon. As each moonball hit the dragon, its body glowed silver as the moonballs dissipated over it. The dragon remained completely still. Its carcass continued to bob up and down, never flinching, not even once. Ever so slowly, like a lifeless cork, the waves washed the dragon's prone remains towards the shore.

"Do you think its dead?" Macey asked.

"I don't know," replied Waldo. "All I know is that I don't trust that thing. It is pure evil, and I wouldn't be surprised if it is simply playing dead whilst it heals itself."

With that thought, Waldo threw several more moonballs. All of which were direct hits on the dragon, but still there was no visible reaction from the dragon.

"Let's not wait around here. Let's go back to the resort and watch it from there," Waldo suggested.

"OK," replied Macey.

Waldo and Macey ran back along the beach and back to their room where they watched the Red Dragon from their window. They watched it for over an hour, as the sea slowly washed it towards the shore. Finally, it was washed up onto the beach. It didn't move. Waldo kept a close eye on it all day, but it just lay lifeless on the beach, as the waves washed around it.

The dragon drew a good deal of attention to it, as word passed around the resort about it being washed up on the beach. It wasn't long before a crowd of onlookers gathered around. They were very cautious at first, but then as they became more and more brave they moved closer and closer. Finally, someone plucked up the courage and crawled on top of the dragon and was sitting on the dragon's neck with his fist raised triumphantly. Still the dragon remained lifeless and still. There were no signs of it breathing, and all who were near it were convinced that the dragon was truly dead. Waldo sighed with relief when he saw it was true.

Waldo exclaimed "Look Macey. The dragon is really dead!" He pointing out the window to the crowd on the beach making mockery of it. Macey looked, "So many lives and so many lands has this dragon destroyed," she said. "Come Waldo, let's eat lunch." She took him by the hand, and they went to the Grand Dining room where they ate a hearty meal of exotic delights. Most of the time they were not entirely sure what they were eating, yet whatever it was, the food certainly did taste exquisite.

After lunch, Waldo and Macey returned to their room and had another spa bath. They kissed each other passionately, and then they kissed some more until eventually they retired in their bed were they lay quite exhausted, and fell asleep. The afternoon suns were shining brightly outside. After an hour or two, Waldo woke up. Macey looked so beautiful and peaceful when she was asleep, and he loved watching her when she was sleeping. He watched her for a while, and then walked over to the window to see what was happening on the beach. The crowds had gone, and the lifeless dragon was still on the sand. The tide had gone out, and the dragon was now beached on dry sand high above the water line. Waldo looked over to Macey, who was sound asleep on the bed. Her eyelids were quivering in short spasms, so he knew that she was dreaming. Sweet dreams, he thought, as she smiled in her sleep.

Waldo decided that he wouldn't wake Macey, but he would go and take a closer look at the dragon. Maybe it had an orb, although he doubted it would still be there given so many onlookers. So off he went down to the beach alone. He walked up to the dragon cautiously, but it clearly wasn't breathing. Its eyes were glazed open, and its lifeless body lay heavy on the sand. As Waldo walked behind the great hulk of the beast, out of sight of the dragon's eyes, the dragon blinked.

The dragon was alive! The twin suns had been pouring replenishing sun light upon the dragon all day, and its bright-red scales had sucked up the life-giving energy, and used it to rapidly heal itself. As Waldo walked behind the dragon, he stepped over its tail, and as he was walking back around towards its head again, its huge tail raised silently behind Waldo's head, poised to strike.

Waldo suddenly heard Macey calling out to him from afar. She was jumping up and down and waving her arms madly. Waldo smiled and waved back at her. His hand was raised high in the sky as he waved to her and smiled. The dragon struck! Macey saw the great tail of the dragon whip around and strike Waldo across the back of his head. Waldo fell unconscious on the sand. Macey was frozen on the spot with the horror of it all . . . the Red Dragon raised its gigantic bulk. It then picked Waldo up in its clawed feet and raised itself into the air. Macey could do nothing but watch. The Red Dragon flapped its wings and lifted Waldo with it as it flew away. It shimmered and Waldo, and the dragon disappeared. They were gone!

Macey's heart raced. She was shocked, confused, and in a panic. What could she do? She walked around in a circle shaking her clenched fists up and down as her mind raced . . . then she remembered and clasped her bracelet. The Great Book sensing her trauma scanned her thoughts for what was stressing her. Macey was gibbering incoherently as the tears streamed down her face. The Great Book transported her back to the Pedestal of Light whilst summoning Miadrag. When the Dragon arrived, Macey was still gibbering. The dragon entered Macey's mind, and as he sifted through her memory, he could re-live the terrible moments of Waldo's capture by the Red Dragon.

Miadrag comforted Macey with a soothing voice in her head. She tried hard to calm herself down, but she was very upset, and she was crying. Her heart was racing with anxious thoughts. Not knowing what to do and her visible distress was frighteningly disturbing to both the Book and Miadrag. The dragon listened intently to Macey's inner voice and soothed her panic for some time before she could compose herself. When Macey had calmed down enough Miadrag spoke out loud. "Mmmm . . . ," he began. "If the Red Dragon meant to hurt Waldo, he would have already done so, so it is more likely that he wanted him alive." Miadrag paused as he thought some more, "He must be taking him to the Salimandé. No doubt the dragon will be hoping that the Salimandé will be most pleased, and that they might be able to re-unite and return to their evil ways."

Macey questioned, "But what then Miadrag? What will they do to Waldo?" Macey was able to compose her thoughts and speak much more clearly now. "We both know the true answer to that Macey. I can only tell you that Waldo is still alive, as I can still feel his life force flowing strongly within the Source of Life."

"Great book, can you transport Waldo back?" asked Miadrag.

The Book replied, "Alas, I have tried, but I am afraid the band has been removed from Waldo's wrist, for only the band returned."

"Do you know where they have taken him?" Miadrag asked.

"The band returned from the planet Arachno. It is an inhospitable planet in the outer reaches of the worlds of the first dimension. It lies at the very edge of our universe," replied the Great Book.

"Then what are you waiting for—transport me now!" growled the dragon.

"I am coming with you," insisted Macey.

"Don't be so hasty," insisted the Book. "This will be very dangerous. Better you stay here Macey."

"No!" Macey replied sternly, "I command you, send me with Maiadrag now!"

The Book responded, "Very well your highness, but first we must prepare you for the battle that you both shall surely find there."

The book materialised a sword and shield. "Macey, take this shield and this sword. The shield will protect you from the red dragons' breath and when you hold this sword before you, it will deflect all the evil that the Salimandé may throw at you. The armour I will give you, will also protect you from anything that might strike you." The Book then materialised the sword and shield into Macey's hands. Then the Book materialised the armour onto her body. Macey was now standing before them in full battle attire. The frosted silver armour had a shining silver shield with the crest of the Maligrandé in the middle of it. The same crest was panelled on the shining chest plate in her armour. The shield and sword also held the marks of the Maligrandé engraved on them. They were surprisingly light, as they were made of pure titanium, and they were polished like a silver mirror so that they shone like the moon itself. Macey's armour was made of a fine weaved titanium mesh. It was very light and flexible, and extremely comfortable. In fact, Macey could barely discern the difference between the armour, and her natural skin.

"There," said the book quite satisfied with itself. "You are ready."

The dragon questioned, "Umm . . . Macey, have you ever used a weapon before?"

Macey looked afraid. "No, Miadrag, I've never held a sword before in my life," she exclaimed.

The dragon exclaimed both impatiently and angrily, "Book!"

"Oh yes," said the Book. "Nearly forgot . . . the master training sequence."

Suddenly, Macey's body was lifted prone into the air as a great beam of light flooded her body. It re-programmed the neural links between her mind and body. Macey was given the courage and strength of ancient warriors past. She was also given the abilities and speed of a Kung Fu master, and the skill and agility with a sword, of a Jedi Knight. The process took only a few minutes and Macey was gently returned to the ground.

The Book enquired, "How do you feel now Macey?" Macey swirled the sword in a flurry of barely visible circles. She arched her body backwards and performed a perfect double back flip and landed in a stance with the sword poised ready to strike.

She said fiercely as she maintained her threatening poise, "I am ready!"

Miadrag raised his eyelid in astonishment as he said, "Impressive!"

"One final thing," said the book as he materialised Waldo's transgression band into Macey's hand, "When you find Waldo, make sure you give him this," Macey nodded knowingly.

At that, the Great Book immediately transported Miadrag and Macey to Waldo's last known position, on the distant planet of Arachno.

Conquest of the Warrior Queen

fter the dragon had seized Waldo, and shimmered away it soon reappeared in the skies over the dark barren wastelands of the rocky planet Arachno. As they flew, the land was dark and devoid of vegetation beneath them. It was crawling with the most hideous of giant bugs that swarmed and scurried quickly over the land. One particularly nasty flying bug spotted the dragon and flew after it. As it neared, the dragon turned and blew a great rally of flames that incinerated it instantly. Its burning carcass fell to the dark rocky ground beneath, where it busted open in a splash of orange-yellow sludge on impact. It lay lifeless on the rocks below. Orange-yellow sludge continued to ooze out of it.

Arachno was the perfect place for the source of all evil to call home. Nothing could live here undetected by the scourge of hideous flesh eating bugs. They scavenged all across the land in large numbers. The Salimandé used the great bug army for protection. In return, he would provide them an endless supply of human hosts. The bugs needed human hosts to breed. They lay their eggs inside the live hosts, and use them initially as incubators to keep the eggs warm until they hatch, and then as live food for their young. It was an unthinkable symbiosis that raised evilness and cruelty to new extremes.

The Salimandé had taken residence in a deserted, dark, dingy castle, that sat a top of a jagged mountain face. It was drenched in a single beam of sunlight that cut threw a permanent hole in the otherwise completely overcast skies in this always dreary place. The castle's walls were a cold dark stone that stretched skyward in eerie pointed stone spires. It painted the most black, cold and sinister of silhouettes. Indeed, the castle looked as evil as its inhabitants inside. Its appearance screamed out—warning, stay away, run for your lives!

The Red Dragon shimmered into the castle. He materialised before the Salimandé. The Red Dragon humbly approached the Salimandé and presented his peace offering of Waldo's still unconscious body. The Salimandé was delighted. When they were together their strength grew stronger, and they could feel it. They relished in how good it was to feel the power again flowing through them. They made a new pact, and a new alliance was formed. The forces of evil grew strong.

The Salimandé now hovering over Waldo's limp body as it lay on the floor in front of him, was indeed well pleased. He had an evil plan to be rid of Waldo, once and for all. A plan that would delight him in its slow and gruesome despatch, of Waldo's miserable life. He delighted in the dragon and praised him. The re-uniting of the Salimandé and the Red Dragon completed the Source of Evil once more. The power of the evil duo began to replenish, and as they became stronger and stronger their evilness spread. Their emanating power caused the suns above to shine even more brightly so that the single sun beam streaming downward upon the castle, was more intense, in turn giving them more power. The contrast of the black castle shining in the bright light, reflected an even deeper blackness across the land before it. I was indeed a sinister sight to behold!

The Salimandé walked over to Waldo, picked up his limp head in his hands and sneered in the most sinister and gravely of voices, "Take him to the pit!" Waldo was taken to a dark damp room somewhere deep in the dungeons beneath the castle, and tied up on a large rack in the centre of a room. The crystal band around his wrist was removed, and thrown as far away as possible, across the floor of the large cavernous room.

The pit was a large circular room entirely encased in rock. It had a jagged rock ceiling. It's cold walls, and floors were made of smooth polished rock. It was an enormous arena, some twenty meters high and eighty meters across. On one, side was a maze of large round caverns that led off into a labyrinth of darkness. On the other side was a barrier of thick iron bars and behind the barrier were seats, set so they sloped back, so that spectators watching, could enjoy an uninterrupted view of the events taking place before them.

Waldo regained consciousness. He surveyed his surrounds. Waldo thought to himself, "Great . . . another one of the Salimandés' blood-curdling arenas . . . and judging from that viewing barrier. This must be where he gets his jollies from watching some poor retch being torn to threads as they are eaten alive by lions," Waldo was mostly right . . . well all except the bit about the lions, as lions would have been much better than what Arachno had to offer.

The Salimandé and the Dragon shimmered down to the arena in order to watch the spectacle that was about to take place. Waldo was struggling to get free. He conjured a moonball and let it fly at the guards, but he missed as his hands were tied fast to the rack. The guards quickly came up from behind the rack, grabbed Waldo's head and forced his mouth open from behind. They poured a bad tasting fluid down his throat. Waldo immediately spat most of it out, but the remnants of the poison were quickly absorbed into his blood stream. This was a very nasty poison. It was extracted from the Manarcho bug. These were the bugs that were swarming all over Arachno.

The name Manarcho comes from the words Mantis and Arachno. The Manarcho's poison is an immobilising poison. It is used by the bug to paralyse the muscles in the body of its prey. It was a particularly sinister poison because whilst it completely paralysed its victims, it also left them with full consciousness and with complete feeling. Death by Manarcho is excruciatingly slow and extremely distressing for the victim. Firstly, the adult Manarcho lays its eggs in the host's living body, a painful enough process in itself. The eggs incubate using the body's warmth, and usually hatch after a few days. Over the next few weeks, the hatchlings live off of the host. They nibble at the living flesh, until eventually the host dies, but they ensure that will take as long as possible, in order to keep the flesh fresh, for as long as they can.

The poison worked quickly on Waldo's body. No matter how hard Waldo tried he could no longer move, not even to blink. The guards brought in a wooden box and placed it on the floor about ten meters in front of Waldo. They opened it. Inside the box was a concoction of many strange things, but included rotting flesh and blood. It gave off a powerful and rancid odour that smelt like a mixture of rotting meat and decaying beetles.

They took some of the smelly concoction, and smeared it on Waldo's clothes. The smell was over bearing. The guards then quickly retreated to safety behind the iron barrier. The rancid smell wafted around the arena. The Salimandé conjured an ill wind. It blew the smell down the dark caverns and deep inside the rock to the Manarcho hive below. After a few minutes, there was a scurrying noise. It sounded like hard pointed claws scurrying over rock. The caverns were behind Waldo, so he couldn't see what was venturing out, but he could hear and smell them. There was a great tumult as two giant bugs entered and started to fight. It was a territorial fight to the death. The Salimandé and the Red Dragon were delighted. The guards cheered and egged on the fight. To the victor, would go the spoils. Unfortunately, the prize was Waldo—soon to be a living egg sack!

As the vicious fight between the bugs went on for a further fifteen minutes, the Salimandé and the other spectators were utterly excited. Their exhilaration grew. Finally, one of the Manarcho managed to strike a winning blow on the other. The loser rose up in the air, and then crashed to the floor, severely wounded. It scurried off down one of the caverns. The victor made its way over to the box in front of Waldo, and as it studied the box's contents, Waldo got to see what he was dealing with . . . and oh—it was horrible! Waldo tried to conjure a moonball, moon beams and even moon light. He tried to levitate, everything and anything he could think of, but nothing worked. The potion was too strong. He was beside himself with horror. Waldo was powerless. He wished he was facing lions.

The giant bug turned and faced Waldo. It was attracted to Waldo's smell. It was well aware that there was a human host waiting for it there. It scurried over and was suddenly upon Waldo—face-to-face! It was like nothing he had ever seen before. It was all black. Its body was encased by its highly polished hard black armour. It had a frightening bright-red stripe down the third segment of its body. This segment was shaped like the rear section of a Praying Mantis. It had large black Mantis wings folded along its sides. The head and middle sections were that of a spider. It had two rows of four eyes, and long sharp fangs that extended out of huge red sacks above the jagged teeth in its mouth. The fangs dripped with poison. They were shiny and hard, long and thin, and they tapered into extremely sharp points.

The Manarcho reared on its eight hairy legs, just as a funnel web spider does when it flares up, ready to strike. Its fangs were now fully extended with even more poison dripping from them. It was a terrifying sight, and Waldo shuddered inside with the horror of it. Waldo could hear cheers from the stalls. The Salimandé, the dragon and the guards, readied themselves for the spectacle to follow. They relished in excited anticipation. Waldo was about to be pounced on by the Manarcho.

It was at that very moment, that Macey and Miadrag shimmered into the arena. Waldo's heart raced with relief at first and then with extreme anxiety. He was unable to help. Macey would be killed for sure, and he worried that the two had no idea of what they had just shimmered into! Macey and Miadrag were of course horrified at the sight of the flaring Manarcho with its fangs fully extended dripping with poison. Sensing danger the Manarcho leapt at the dragon. It leapt with such speed, there was little time to react, but Maidrag was ready for the Manacrcho. As it flew through the air Miadrag blasted it with a great ball of flames. The Manarcho flew right into the flames where it was incinerated instantly. It fell to the ground in a smouldering heap of ash and shell.

The Salimandé horrified at this turn of events shouted out in a loud voice, "Kill them." The guards poured into the arena with swords and axes drawn. Macey leapt into the air, did a number of successive back flips with her sword blazing. She was fast. Lightening fast! Her sword was accurate and true. It was all a blur to those watching. It was all over in a few seconds. By the time Macey landed back on her feet, poised stationary in a full defensive position ready for anything, the six guards who had entered the arena were lying dead on the floor. At the sight of it, the Salimandé and the Red Dragon, now in a complete rage, both shimmered into the arena. The battle for Waldo—was on once more!

Miadrag immediately leapt onto the back of the Red Dragon. The sound of claws and gnashing teeth accompanied by the thud of giant bodies being swung and flung to the ground filled the air. The roars and thuds from the fighting dragons, echoed loudly around the arena's hollow walls. Flames were blasted in all directions, as the two fought. They were both fighting a fierce battle, with the only likely outcome, being the death of one of them. Meanwhile, the Salimandé was focused on taking care of Macey. "I should have killed you when I had the chance," he said with a cruel scowl. "No matter," the Salimandé continued, "I will kill you now, and then I will feed you and your husband to the Manarcho. Make no mistake, today I will finally be rid of you both, once and for all."

Macey responded, "Bring it on, you bald salami!" The Salimandé was outraged! He conjured a massive fireball. He threw the fireball directly at Macey. Macey stood firm as she braced herself. Her sword held in both hands, poised ready in front of her body. As the ball neared she swung the sword straight and true. It sent the fireball hurtling straight back towards the Salimandé. The fireball was now hurtling back at twice the speed the Salimandé had thrown it at. The Salimandé's eyes were wide with horror. He realised he had no time to avoid being hit. It was coming too fast. He ducked as best he could, but it still hit him side on. He fell to the ground screaming and writhing. The fireball inflicted the most painful of burns. They were etched deep into his right side, right down to the bones, exposing them from his shoulder to his knee. He was very badly wounded. He could barely move. In a flash, Macey was on top of him with her sword wielding. In a flurry of precise arm movements, her sword swirled in circles. She stuck the Salimandé and smashed his left shoulder with her sword. She then knocked him unconscious with a straight blow to the side of his head.

The dragons were still rolling, snapping and snarling, as they blew fire in all directions. Macey barely had time to use her shield to save herself from the Red Dragon's misplaced breath, which was heading straight towards her. The noise was deafening. The dragons roared and tumbled, their claws flaying in all directions. The great commotion they caused, attracted attention from the caves within. Suddenly, there were six Manarcho in the arena. They were now working together, and on the attack, and they looked like they would soon be heading straight for Macey.

Macey ran to Waldo and cut him free. He was stiff. He couldn't move at all. Suddenly, with nothing holding him up, he over balanced and fell stiff as a board towards the stone floor. Waldo had visions of his face being smashed on the cold stone, but Macey suddenly realising what was happening, grabbed him with her lightening reflexes. She managed to rescue him just before he hit the floor. She wrapped her arms around Waldo. Quickly placed his trangression band back on his wrist and dragged his hand to it. Waldo shimmered and was gone. Macey cried out at the top of her voice, "Miadrag! Waldo is safe!" She clasped her hand around her transgression band. The Manarcho was nearly upon her. She exclaimed desperately, "Now book!" Macey, and Miadrag, shimmered and vanished. The Red Dragon was left all alone with the unconscious Salimandé. The attacking Manarcho encircled them, as they closed in on them both.

The Red Dragon turned to defend himself from the angry Manarcho. Suddenly, six more appeared. One of them was already on top of the Salimandé. It had sunk its fangs into the Salimandé and pumped him full of immobilising poison. It then quickly turned and stuck him in the chest with the sting at the end of its body, which it then used to pump its eggs into the Salimandé's limp body. In the meantime, the other eleven Manarcho moved quickly to isolate and surround the Red Dragon. The Red Dragon blew hot flames in a circle. The Manarcho surrounding him were burnt to a smouldering crisp. The burning Manarcho let out cries of agony in a deafening chorus. Their piercing screeches rang out through the caves below, sounding the alarm for the remainder of the swarm to come and defend them. Their hive was under attack!

The Manarcho that had just laid its eggs in the Salimandé's body, quickly picked him up and fled at great speed to the safety of the caves. The dragon saw it scurrying away, and was quick behind it. As the Manarcho disappeared down a nearby cavern, the dragon blew flames after it. The caves were too small for the dragon to follow. The Manarcho was far too quick. It had already turned a corner and disappeared into the depths and the safety of the adjoining caves below.

The dragon was too late. It was furious. It blew flames down the caves for the next hour in a great rage. It continued until it was so exhausted that it was unable to blow flames anymore. There was nothing more that it could do, to save the Salimandé. The Salimandé was lost. He would die the most horrible of deaths. The Salimandé would be eaten alive by the Manarchos' hatching offspring. Ironically the same cruel fate that the Salimandé so hoped to bestow upon Waldo, but for Macey and Miadrag's brave rescue. As soon as the dragon had run out of fire, the Manarcho returned in great numbers. As the angry Manarcho surrounded the dragon, it let out a huge roar, shimmered and disappeared to safety.

New Beginings

ack on Annulus The Great Book was delighted with the safe return of Waldo, Macey and Miadrag. Miadrag was wounded, but he insisted he would be fine given some time healing himself in his lair, so he promptly left so that he could do so. The Great Book raised Waldo's stiffened body into the air. It surrounded him in a great pool of light which it used to extract the deadly poison that was running through Waldo's veins. When the work was done the Book returned Waldo to the ground. Waldo could move again but he and Macey were overcome by the foul stench coming from their clothes, so they both quickly left to shower. Once they were in the shower the maids came and removed their smelly clothes. They lit fragrant oils in the room to remove the remaining smell.

After Macey and Waldo had showered they were both very tired from their ordeal, so they both hopped into bed. Waldo's body was still fighting off the last remnants of the poison, and in his exhausted state he promptly fell asleep. That night Macey was amazed to discover Waldo levitating as the full moon shone through the window. His scar glowed brightly as the Source of Life removed the remaining poison from his body. It also healed the wounds that Waldo had received under the tight grip of the claws of the Red Dragon. Macey sat up all-night and watched over Waldo as he floated above the bed. She was very concerned, and her heart raced as she waited anxiously for him to wake.

As the moon set and Waldo floated back down to the bed, Macey snuggled up to him and held him as he slept. It wasn't long before she too, was fast asleep. It would be mid morning before Macey would be woken by Waldo's stirrings. Waldo gave a huge yawn as he stretched out his arms. He lay on his back in the bed beside Macey. Macey sat up on her side beside him and smiled at him as she bit her lip gently, and gave him a look of love, and anxious concern. She took her finger and delicately tapped him on the end of the nose. Waldo smiled at her. She bent down and kissed him. Waldo kissed her passionately back. "My hero," he said with a cheeky smile, as he mimicked her from the day before.

Macey smiled back at him. "How do you feel?" she asked.

"I feel great," he said as he smiled back at her, and they played with each other's hands.

"I was so worried about you. I really did think that I had lost you, you know."

Waldo replied, "Yeah it was a close one alright. But what about you my Warrior Queen . . . I have never seen anything like that . . . have you been holding out on me?"

Macey replied softly. "No. The Great Book helped me out with some new skills," she smiled. "I am just so glad we were in time to save you."

"Yes . . . . Me too," sighed Waldo softly.

"I had no idea that you would be turning up like that, and wow what a display—your dangerous! It really was the last thing I would have expected," said Waldo merrily. He pulled her to him and kissed her passionately, and she kissed him passionately back, and then they kissed some more . . . Indeed this was a whole new beginning for them, and nothing would be quite the same ever again.

Meanwhile deep in the bowels of the caves back on Arachno, the Manarcho scurried along with its prize of the Salimandé. As it travelled along the caverns, the freshly laid eggs rattled inside the Salimandé. The Manarcho finally entered a chamber deep beneath the ground. It was the main hatchery for the colony. Here, there were dozens of hosts cocooned in a fibrous sticky web that held them upright from the ceiling of the cavern. The Manarcho found a suitable place and spun a web. It hung the Salimandé's cocoon from the ceiling of the cavern, and then left.

From the very minute that the Salimandé was bitten by the Manarcho, he began the fight for life against the fast-acting poison. He drew on the suns above, which shone even brighter in response, as they pumped energy deep below for the Salimandé to use to regain strength. After another day, the Salimandé had gained sufficient strength to be able to concentrate on pushing and expelling the eggs that had been laid inside of him. As he concentrated hard on the eggs. Little by little, the eggs began to work their way out of his body. One by one, the eggs emerged from under his skin, and slowly, and painfully they came out. The eggs were pushed right through the cocoon and onto the ground. There they formed a pile of broken shells at his cocooned feet. The embryos inside the eggs died quickly on the cold stone, as the last steamy wafts of heat left them.

In a few more days the Salimandé had recovered enough to move his arms and legs, at which time, he shimmered and returned once again to his evil lair in the castle above. The Red Dragon was waiting in the vain hope that the Salimandé would somehow return. Their evilness relished in their re-union. Furious in their defeat, yet glorious in their triumph in cheating death, they made their plans to exact an even more horrible revenge. This time their revenge would not be just to destroy Waldo and Macey. Next time, they would destroy everything—including Annulus itself!